P   Singleton,   P9-ELV-607

Stand Up and Cheer

$3.99

DATE DUE

NOV 18 '99	SEP 25 '04		
JAN 25 00	OCT 22 '12		
OCT 19 '01	DEC 10 '12		
OCT 18 '01			
NOV 1 '01			
JAN 10 02			
FEB 18 04			
APR 28 04			
DE 16 04			
MAY 26 06			
SEP 28 06			

LINDA JOY SINGLETON has written nearly twenty young adult and middle grade novels, including the *My Sister, The Ghost* series. While she never was a cheerleader, as a teenager she performed with a round dance group called the Silhouettes. In her twenties, she and her husband, David, square danced professionally with the Rainbow Stars. And as part of her research into cheerleading, she has enrolled in a ballet class.

She lives near Sacramento on three country acres with her husband and two kids, Melissa and Andy. They have lots of animals: dogs, cats, ducks, chickens, goats, and two horses.

STAND UP AND CHEER!

LINDA JOY SINGLETON

AN AVON CAMELOT BOOK

CHEER SQUAD #3: STAND UP AND CHEER! is an original publication of Avon Books. This work has never before appeared in book form.

AVON BOOKS
A division of
The Hearst Corporation
1350 Avenue of the Americas
New York, New York 10019

Copyright © 1996 by Linda Joy Singleton
Excerpt from *Cheer Squad #4: Boys Are Bad News* copyright © 1996 by Linda Joy Singleton
Published by arrangement with the author
Library of Congress Catalog Card Number: 96-96550
ISBN: 0-380-78440-8
RL: 4.5

First Avon Camelot Printing: November 1996

CAMELOT TRADEMARK REG. U.S. PAT. OFF. AND IN OTHER COUNTRIES, MARCA REGISTRADA. HECHO EN U.S.A.

Printed in the U.S.A.

OPM   10 9 8 7 6 5 4 3 2 1

TO A SPECIAL FRIEND,

LINDA BURNS

Who appreciates the finer C.B.'s
of life:

Covered Bridges
Collectible Barbies
and
Children's Books

●●●●●●●●●●●

One

Shoot it!
Sink it in the hoop!
Score! Sharks!
The Sharks rule!

As Tabby Greene listened to the joyous cries from the opposing basketball team, her shoulders slumped and her pompons sagged to her sides. This was Castle Hill Junior High's first basketball game of the season, and their Knights were losing—*badly*.

Tabby stood in front of the bleachers beside the other five cheerleaders and yelled encouraging chants like, "Go, Knights! Fight, Fight, Fight!" or "Dribble it, pass it, we want a basket!" But the Cheer Squad's shouts were lost in the deafening roar of applause as the Silver Creek Sharks scored two more points.

"Another hoop shot for the opposition!" Tabby

groaned to her best friend and Cheer Squad captain Wendi Holcroft. "They're killing us!"

"That's for sure," Wendi agreed, glancing at the scoreboard. "Fifty-four to twenty-four!"

Krystal Carvell gave a toss of her honey-blond ponytail and exclaimed, "Those vicious Sharks are chewing up our team!"

"The game isn't over yet." Anna Herrera, the most optimistic cheerleader at Castle Hill Junior High, flashed a smile. "There's still hope."

"Maybe," Tabby said quietly. Then she crossed her fingers as the Knights' best player, Anna's older brother Esteban, stole the ball from a Shark.

Esteban ran, bounced, and dribbled the ball down the court. He dodged to the left, then sprang to the right, jumping high in the air. But just as he threw the ball, a very tall Shark snatched it away. Another hoop shot for the Sharks—and the referee blew the whistle for a time-out.

Tabby sighed and reminded herself that winning or losing wasn't the most important thing. *But losing feels crummy!* she thought in frustration. *We're supposed to rev up the Knights and rouse them on to a win, but who's going to rev us up?*

"Poor Esteban. He looks really bummed," Krystal said, sinking onto a long wooden bench. She gazed sadly at her tall, dark-haired boyfriend.

"I know how he feels," Rachel Steinberg said sympathetically. Stocky and brown-haired, Rachel was the squad member newest to cheerleading.

2

"Me, too," Celine Jefferson added, slumping on the bench between Rachel and Anna.

"Hey, girls! What's with the glum attitude?" Coach Rusty Laing asked as she strode over. Although she was in her mid-twenties, Coach Laing looked younger: slender, energetic, with a mass of black braids woven with colorful beads cascading around her pretty face.

Tabby pushed back a loose strand of her light-brown hair and shrugged. "I guess we're bummed because our team is being creamed."

Krystal clasped her hands to her chest in a melodramatic gesture. "We're cheering our hearts out, but it's like the Knights don't hear us."

"So cheer louder," Coach Laing urged in a no-nonsense tone. "Get off the bench and whip our team to victory."

"Victory? When we're over thirty points down?" Tabby questioned, mentally calculating the unlikely mathematical odds.

"It's our job to try," Wendi said, jumping up to face her squad. "Come on. Let's spread some cheer."

Coach Laing nodded in approval, then returned to her seat.

Tabby took a deep breath to psych herself up. *Winning doesn't matter,* she reminded herself, *but team spirit does.* Then she hopped off the bench to join Krystal, Anna, Celine, and Rachel as they huddled in a strategic circle around Wendi.

"Smile!" squad captain Wendi ordered. Her silver braces flashed as she grinned. "Show those Sharks that we can have fun no matter what the score is. Let's do the 'Shoot It to the Hoop' chant."

3

"Not *again*," Krystal protested.

"Why not? It's an upbeat routine that we all know well." Wendi gave Krystal a challenging look. Tabby could tell Wendi was annoyed with Krystal. Wendi took her squad captain duties very seriously and expected respect from her teammates.

"But that routine is *so* bor-ring." Krystal rolled her blue eyes. "Let's jazz up the crowd with some stunts. Like a herkie or a basket toss."

"We haven't practiced those moves enough," Wendi objected. "We can't risk an injury."

"I won't get hurt," Krystal said with a confident tilt to her head. "But if you don't want to do stunts, let's start a crowd chant of Esteban's name. He's the team's best player. He just needs some encouragement."

"So go over and encourage him," Celine teased, puckering her lips in a "kiss" pantomime. "He's *your* guy, not ours."

"You're just jealous because I'm the only girl on the squad with a boyfriend," Krystal fired back.

"As if I cared!" Celine said, her black eyes flashing.

"Time out," Wendi said firmly, quickly stepping between Krystal and Celine. "Let's see some teamwork."

But Krystal and Celine crossed their arms and turned away from each other. Wendi looked on in frustration, clearly unsure how to handle this situation.

Tabby figured the tension of the game was putting her friends on edge. Trying to help, Tabby said calmly, "Hey, the players are counting on us, and they aren't the only ones." She pointed toward the bleachers. "Just look up there. Celine, isn't your grandmother watching?"

"Yeah." Celine smoothed back her ebony hair. "Gram is the greatest." Celine's mother had been in a coma for nearly six months following a tragic bus accident, and her grandmother tried to make up for her mother being in the hospital.

"Maybe your mother will be better by our regional competition," Krystal said, her mood quickly changing from angry to sympathetic. "But at least your grandmother is here. My parents are, too—and they don't usually come to school games."

"My family hardly ever misses a game," Wendi said. "Mom, Dad, and my sister Valerie are in the second row. My parents spent years watching Valerie perform cheers, but now it's my turn and I really want to impress them."

"So let's impress them and everyone else," Tabby urged, glad that her friends were acting like a team again.

"You said it, Tabby!" Anna gave an enthusiastic nod. "Rachel's parents are sitting with my family, and I know they're all behind us one hundred percent."

Tabby grinned at Anna's words, but when she glanced up at the bleachers her grin faded. Wendi, Anna, Krystal, Celine, and Rachel had family supporting them—but Tabby had no one.

Suddenly, Tabby felt alone and abandoned. Her mother worked most evenings and couldn't attend games. Adam, Tabby's older brother, was busy with his high-school activities. And Tabby's divorced father simply wasn't interested. He lived thirty miles away and worked as a college football coach. Despite his busy schedule, he went to most of Adam's games—but he'd never attended any of Tabby's recitals, plays, or cheerleading events.

"Come on, squad. Show some spirit!" Wendi said with a rousing wave of her poms.

"Yeah!" Tabby encouraged.

Wendi tossed Tabby a grateful look, then faced the whole squad. "Let's show everyone we can act like winners. Krystal's right about the 'Shoot It' chant being boring. So let's try the new routine we've been practicing—the Superstar."

Tabby and her friends waved their poms in excited agreement. Then the six cheerleaders cartwheeled, jumped, and flipped to the middle of the gym. They made a six-pointed star with one pom reaching high to form a colorful spinning star and the other hand down at their sides. Applause went up from the Castle Hill bleachers as the Cheer Squad chanted:

S-U-P-E-R . . . *Superstars,*
The Knights are superstars,
Shoot, pass, and dribble,
Making balls fly, into the sky,
Past the moon—as high as Mars.
S-U-P-E-R . . . *Superstars,*
The knights are super-duper,
Shooting Stars!

Tabby felt energized as she jumped and waved her poms high over her head. An earthquake of foot-stomping, hand-clapping enthusiasm rocked the floors and bleachers. Then the referee blew the whistle.

6

The game was back on!

Tabby stood beside her friends and cheered wildly when a few seconds later Esteban scored a fantastic three-point shot. This seemed to spur the Knights to sink more baskets. The points mounted up quickly. The Knights were truly shooting stars.

Near the end of fourth quarter, the score was 57 to 59. The Sharks were still ahead, but now they were starting to look tense.

Esteban stole the ball and dribbled it toward the hoop.

Krystal jumped up and cried out, "Shoot the ball, Esteban! Go, Esteban!"

Tabby waved her poms and joined in. Soon the Castle Hill bleachers echoed with Esteban's name. Tabby hadn't felt this jazzed since last month when the Cheer Squad had competed in the Harvest Festival Talent Show—maybe not even then! Her throat ached from screaming, but she was past caring. *Win, win!* her mind shouted. *Come on, Esteban, you can do it!*

Mere seconds were left and Esteban's fingers danced with the ball; spinning pirouettes and defying gravity. Suddenly his arm sprang up and the ball sailed toward the net ... closer, closer, over the net, down to the rim—but it hit the backboard and bounced away.

The Sharks went crazy.

The Knights stood in stunned shock, and the Cheer Squad's poms drooped like wilted flowers to their sides.

"Poor Esteban," Krystal murmured.

"Esteban tried hard," Wendi said, patting Krystal on the shoulder. "I'm proud of our team.

The Knights played a good game. Next time they'll win."

Yeah, next time, Tabby thought, feeling hopeful for the basketball players, the Cheer Squad, and the loyal Knights fans.

Tabby's gaze swept over the bleachers, lingering on the familiar faces of her friends' families. Celine's tawny-skinned, black-haired grandmother; Wendi's gorgeous sister Valerie; Krystal's father; and Anna's large family. So many supportive faces, all ready to give encouraging pep talks and loving praise.

But I don't have any family watching me, Tabby thought with a frown. *Maybe Mom can make it to my next—*

Suddenly Tabby gasped.

She stared in astonishment at a figure rising from the back of the bleachers. A robust, middle-aged man with receding sandy hair and distinguished-looking glasses. Someone Tabby knew well ... but it couldn't be! It wasn't possible!

Tabby's emotions skyrocketed and her heart pounded with disbelief as she gazed at the last person in the world she expected to see here.

●●●●●●●●●●●●

Two

"DAD!" Tabby cried, dropping her poms and rushing up the bleachers. She met her father halfway and hugged him. She still couldn't believe he was actually *here*—but she was thrilled!

"Surprised to see me?" Mr. Greene asked, giving a playful tug on Tabby's ponytail.

"Surprised is an understatement!" Tabby admitted.

"You did some terrific moves out there. I had a great time watching." Mr. Greene squeezed her hand. "Not that anything could have kept me away. Not after I heard what a fine athlete you'd become."

"Huh?" Tabby wrinkled her brow. "What do you mean?"

"Your mother told me the great news. Blew me away, too. Good work!" he said in the brisk, clipped manner he probably used with the football players he coached.

"Great news?" Tabby felt confused.

"Show some enthusiasm, Tabby." Her father

chuckled. "Not every junior high cheerleading squad is up to serious competition."

"Oh, the regionals." Tabby smiled, beginning to understand. The Cheer Squad would be competing against other junior highs in just over two weeks. Tabby couldn't wait.

"I've watched college cheerleaders in action and it's darned hard work," her father went on. "Takes a lot of sweat, talent, and practice. I admire that. Way to go, Tabby."

"Really? Does that mean you'll come to the regionals?" Tabby asked with a hesitant smile. Her father usually saved his enthusiasm for winning touchdowns and macho sports talk with Adam. He'd never shown any interest in her activities—until now.

"You bet I'll be there." Mr. Greene squeezed Tabby's hand. "And I'll bring my camera to shoot photos of your first-place trophy."

"First place?" Tabby repeated wistfully. "That would be great, but I'd be happy with second or third."

"Always aim for the top. Don't settle for anything but the best. You can do it. You're my girl."

Tabby beamed. *Daddy's girl.* Something she'd always wanted to be, but only in her most secret dreams. "Okay, Dad. I'll do my best to win. But now I want you to meet my coach." Tabby tugged on his arm. "Come on. You'll like Coach Laing. She's the coolest."

Tabby proudly led her father down the bleachers, to the court where Coach Laing chatted with several cheerleaders and their families. Heads turned in surprise when Tabby introduced her father. Tabby still couldn't believe he was actually *here*—not with Adam the favorite, but with *her*.

And things got even better when Coach Laing suggested the squad and their families go out for pizzas. "To celebrate a fun, spirited game," Rusty Laing declared with high enthusiasm.

A short time later, Tabby happily chewed on a warm, cheesy pizza with pepperoni and sausage. Beside her, Mr. Greene reached for his second slice of pizza. Laughter, teasing, and fun conversation spilled around the long wooden table. No one watching would ever guess that this happy group had just *lost* a basketball game.

"Fine squad you got here," Mr. Greene told Rusty Laing, who sat across from him. "The girls respect you. That says a lot for your work."

"Actually, the girls and I are still adjusting to each other," Coach Laing explained honestly. "I've only been coaching the Cheer Squad for a few weeks."

"Ah—a rookie." Mr. Greene's tanned face spread into a grin. "You hang in there. Coaching is a tough job, but the kids are worth it."

"Dad is a coach, too." Tabby flashed a proud smile. "He coaches football at Valley Community College. He led the Volcanoes into three winning seasons."

"I'm impressed," Miss Laing said as she dabbed her mouth with a napkin. "It's great you took time out from your busy schedule to watch Tabby. I appreciate support from the parents."

"I'm always eager to support fine athletes," Mr. Greene declared. "And these girls are winners if I ever saw 'em. I predict the Cheer Squad will go a long ways."

"All the way to the nationals, I hope," Miss Laing agreed with a grin. "But first we have to do well in the regionals. That's when the girls will get their first taste of real competition."

"To win they'll have to buckle down and put in extra practice hours." Mr. Greene pursed his lips together. "And if you don't mind my saying so, seems like you're not using all your resources."

"What do you mean?" Coach Laing asked, her beaded braids rattling softly as she tilted her head to give Tabby's father a puzzled look.

"Competition is more than perfecting a winning routine," Mr. Greene said, putting down his slice of pizza. "It's travel, uniforms, music arrangements, and a million details. Preparation and paperwork can bog you down when you need to practice the most. There's only one solution."

"What?" Coach Laing asked.

"Call in the troops. Recruit extra help."

Anna said, "My Aunt Carlotta is our advisor and she helps out a lot."

"That's a start." Mr. Greene nodded his approval. "But why not pool other parents and relatives into a support group? A booster club."

"Awesome idea!" Coach Laing exclaimed.

Other parents jumped in the conversation and soon a lively discussion spread around the long table. Everyone offered ideas and support. Wendi's sister, Celine's grandmother, Anna's parents, and even Krystal's busy parents were enthusiastic.

Tabby just listened in amazement. Her father—the man who usually just kissed her on the cheek as he breezed out the door with Adam—

was actually making plans to help her cheerleading squad. That meant spending time with *her*.

I can't believe this is happening, Tabby thought, torn between happiness and doubt. She remembered all the times her father had disappointed her in the past. *But this time will be different,* she reassured herself. *Dad won't let me down. I'm sure of it.*

"Your father actually showed up?" Mrs. Greene asked in disbelief that evening. She still wore her white nursing uniform from Haven Convalescent Home, and her face was marked with tired lines, making her appear older than her thirty-eight years.

Tabby sat up straight in bed, put her Julie Sutton Mystery novel aside, and gave a confident nod. "Dad not only watched my game, but he organized a parents' booster club. He really wants to get involved and help out."

"You can't be serious!"

"But I am," Tabby insisted. She refused to let doubt ruin her happy evening. Being "Daddy's girl" had felt wonderful.

Mrs. Greene rubbed her chin thoughtfully. "And your father is starting a booster club? I find that hard to believe."

"Believe it, Mom. Dad even made plans to come to some of my cheerleading practices next week."

"Don't count on it," her mother warned. "Alex is famous for making promises just so he can break them. When it comes to family, he's just not the responsible type."

Tabby's happiness began to slip away. Her parents had been divorced for three years and her mother was still bitter. Mom was too tired to date, and spent all her spare time with her kids.

"Dad *is* interested in me," Tabby said defensively. "He even promised to drive me to the regional competition."

"Then he better keep his word. I'd drive you myself, but I'm scheduled to work that Saturday."

"Dad won't cancel. He can be responsible when he wants to."

"Of course he can," Mrs. Greene said, sounding sad. "And he's terrific with Adam. I'm happy he's finally realizing he has a wonderful, talented daughter, too. I just wish . . ." She sat on the corner of her bed and sighed. "I just wish I could be there more for you and Adam."

"You do the best you can," Tabby said quickly. "You took time off so you could come to our haunted house. And you were at the Harvest Festival."

Mrs. Greene ran her fingers across her short curly dark hair. "I try, honey."

"I know, and I appreciate it." Tabby hugged her mother. "You're the best, Mom."

After her mother left, Tabby tried to finish reading her mystery, but it was hard to concentrate. She kept thinking about her parents. Maybe it was childish, but she had a wild hope that they'd get back together someday.

I feel so confused sometimes, she thought, staring up at the shadows on her ceiling. *I may have a high IQ, but when it comes to my own life, I don't know any of the answers. Why can't I have a warm, loving family like Wendi? Mom works too hard and isn't very happy. Adam seems ob-*

sessed with sports and his friends. And Dad has never paid much attention to me . . . until today. But I can't help but worry he'll lose interest and forget about me all over again.

Sighing, Tabby picked up her book, this time reading through to the end. Once again Julie Sutton, girl detective, successfully pieced together puzzling clues and unmasked a dangerous killer. Murder solved.

Fictional detectives solve problems so easily, Tabby mused, starting to feel sleepy. *I wish I were a teenage sleuth. I'd love to investigate a real mystery. And while I was at it, I'd solve my parents' problems, too. Then we could be a happy family once again.*

Tabby's eyelids drooped and she reached over to snap off her bedside light. *As she drifted off toward slumber, two words echoed in her mind over and over: "I wish."*

•••••••••••
Three

Tabby was enjoying a wonderful dream about the regional competition. She wore her new green-and-gold uniform, held gold poms in one hand, and a gleaming first-place trophy in the other. Her father hugged and congratulated her as he proudly snapped pictures.

There was a sharp noise and a bright flash as Tabby's bedroom light was snapped on. Tabby's eyes flew open and she bolted up in bed. "What? Who?"

"The bananas are missing!" a medium-tall figure exclaimed, striding into Tabby's room.

"Huh?" Tabby rubbed her eyes and stared groggily at her older brother. "Adam? What do you want?"

"A banana for my sack lunch," he said impatiently.

Broad-shouldered, muscular fifteen-year-old Adam looked comical with uncombed light-brown hair, a wrinkled black T-shirt, and a flustered expression. Tabby couldn't help but giggle.

"This is no laughing matter," Adam said roughly. "It's bad enough I got to make my own lunch since Mom started working evenings. Now I can't find any fruit. Where are the bananas?"

"At the grocery store," Tabby teased. "In the produce section."

"Funny," Adam said sarcastically. "My ride's gonna show any minute. And I can't make my lunch if I can't even find a crummy banana."

Tabby rolled her eyes. Adam was so disorganized. It was amazing he managed to dress himself. "Check the bread box. That's where Mom puts fruit sometimes. If you ever helped clean up around here, you'd know that."

"I got better things to do. I have to bulk up for my wrestling meets. And there's a Winter Bowl benefit football game coming up so I got to work out with the team." Adam crossed his arms and added, "You should help Mom more since you're not doing anything important."

"Anything important!" Tabby cried, jumping out of bed to face her brother with an outraged expression. "For your information, my cheerleading is so important that Dad came to watch me last night."

"No way."

"He did so. Dad was at the basketball game."

"Dad was here in town?" Adam's jaw dropped. "But he didn't say anything about it to me."

"I'm telling the truth. Dad is even organizing a Cheer Squad parents' booster club."

"I don't believe it. Dad is a macho guy. Why would he bother with cheerleaders?"

"Because he's *my* father, too," Tabby said, feeling a rush of anger at her brother. "Unlike you,

Mr. Male Chauvinist Jock, Dad respects cheerleaders."

"I don't have anything against cheerleaders. My last girlfriend cheered for our team. And she was one fine babe."

Tabby pursed her lips in annoyance. "This isn't the Dark Ages, Adam. Girls shouldn't be called 'babe' and cheerleading isn't a popularity or beauty contest. Dad called us talented athletes."

"Yeah, right," Adam snorted. "What's athletic about wearing short skirts and waving pompoms?"

"The word is pom*pon*." Tabby put her hands on her hips and lashed out, "You don't have a clue about *my* sport. We have to practice as much— maybe more—than you do. We do complicated stunts, gymnastic moves, and all kinds of dance steps. And Dad thinks our squad is good enough to win a first-place trophy at the regional competition in two weeks."

"Two weeks!" Adam stared at Tabby for a moment, his hazel eyes narrowed and his mouth set in an angry line. "You don't know what you're talking about. Just forget I ever came in here. I can find my own banana!" Then he strode out of the room.

"Brothers!" Tabby murmured to herself. Then she immediately felt guilty and regretted blowing up at Adam. This was definitely not the way to create a happy family.

A short time later, Tabby was dressed and ready for school. She grabbed her backpack, then started to leave her room. But she hesitated when she realized it was Thursday, which meant cheerleading practice after school. So she detoured into the apartment's compact laundry room where she'd left the duffle bag that held her poms, sneakers, shorts, and T-shirt. Then she headed for the kitchen.

Breakfast at the Greene house was a quiet event. Adam had already left by the time Tabby poured milk over her cereal. And Tabby's mother was still sleeping.

It was a relief to reach school where there was lots of noise, friendly waves, and activity. Tabby grinned when she saw Wendi waiting by their side-by-side lockers. *Some kids may hate going to school,* Tabby thought, *but not me. School feels more like home than home does.*

As Tabby neatly placed her duffle bag in her locker, Wendi talked excitedly about the parents' booster club.

"My parents are really eager to help our squad," Wendi said. "I haven't seen them this hyped since Valerie cheered in the nationals."

"Only it's nicer now because *you're* the cheerleader in the family," Tabby said warmly.

"Which feels great." Wendi hugged her backpack to her chest. "I've been dreaming of cheering forever. Remember all those times I dragged you into the backyard and we borrowed Valerie's pompons and pretended to be cheerleaders?"

"How could I forget?" Tabby said teasingly. "Especially that time I threw Valerie's poms so high in the air they got stuck in a tree."

"And when I climbed the tree to get them, I ripped my shorts," Wendi said, giggling. "We had a lot of fun playing cheerleader. And now we *are* cheerleaders. It's hard to believe it's finally happened."

"You made it happen." Tabby flashed a warm smile. "Darlene Dittman may have kept you off the squad in sixth grade, but you kept on trying and trying—until you succeeded."

"We succeeded together," Wendi said as they left the lockers.

Tabby's smile widened. *Together*—that's the way best friends should always be. Then they both waved and headed for their separate homeroom classes.

For the next few hours, Tabby's head was too filled with complicated equations, hypothetical concepts, and sentence structures to think about cheerleading. But when her fourth-period class ended, she raced to join her cheerleading friends at lunch.

Usually the Cheer Squad sat outside, but the weather had turned chilly and they were forced to crowd into the cafeteria. Tabby dropped her backpack on the table where Anna and Krystal sat, then joined Wendi in the hot-lunch line.

After getting a tray of mixed vegetables, a stale roll, and a mysterious meat covered with puke-brown gravy, Tabby and Wendi headed toward the table where Anna and Krystal sat. As they passed the table where the Castle Hill Cheerleaders were gathered, Tabby heard giggles.

"It's no surprise the basketball team lost yesterday," Darlene Dittman, the striking white-blond squad captain, said in a deliberately loud voice. "Not with the Klutz Squad cheering for them."

Black-haired, cocoa-skinned LaShaun cackled. "The Cheer Squad is an embarrassment to our school."

Darlene nodded. "They should do everyone a favor and quit."

Tabby bit her lip to hold her temper. It was no secret that Darlene resented their squad. And that resentment had grown worse since the Cheer Squad won third place at the Harvest Festival while the Castle Hill Cheerleaders came in fifth.

"Those creeps!" Wendi hissed, looking angry enough to throw her food tray at Darlene and LaShaun. "I should tell them—"

"No!" Tabby said firmly. "Don't say anything. Let's just walk calmly by and pretend we didn't hear."

Wendi's face reddened, nearly matching her auburn hair. "But that witch called us the Klutz Squad. We can't ignore it."

Darlene whispered something to a brunette cheerleader named Kayla, which made Kayla's eyes grow wide with astonishment. "You mean they had the nerve to enter the regionals?" Kayla asked incredulously.

"Outrageous, isn't it?" Darlene responded with a laugh.

"That's it!" Wendi exploded, stomping her foot. Then before Tabby could stop her, she strode over to face Darlene. "Cut out the insults!"

"Just telling it like it is," Darlene said smugly. "Your squad has no business entering the regionals. Competition is for *real* cheerleaders—like us."

"Fifth place isn't something to brag about," Wendi retorted.

"That was just a fluke," Darlene scoffed. "A small-time talent show with small-time judges.

At the regionals, the judges will be professionals. They'll recognize our talent and your lack of it."

"You think so?" Wendi challenged. "Well think again, because the Cheer Squad is going to win in the performance cheer division."

Darlene lifted her chin haughtily. "Only if they offer a booby prize for mismatched poms and tacky uniforms."

Wendi gave a slow smile. "For your information, our squad has *new* uniforms complete with matching poms."

Tabby quietly stood behind Wendi, her anger at the Castle Hill girls growing. She was tempted to dump her puke-brown gravy on Darlene's perfect blond head. Unfortunately, she knew that wouldn't solve anything.

"Your squad is only entering *one* division?" LaShaun taunted after taking a sip from her small carton of Plum Berry Punch. "We're competing in *two*."

"Yeah," Kayla added. "The same one as you and—"

"Don't tell them!" Darlene cupped her hand over Kayla's mouth. "Our second division is a secret. And with the professional trainers Dad's hired to work with us, the Castle Hill cheerleaders are sure to win in both divisions."

"Yeah. Performance cheer and . . . the other one," LaShaun added.

"My father says the cost of success is unimportant," Darlene boasted. "He'll do whatever it takes to help us win."

"We have lots of help, too," Tabby said, proudly thinking of her own father.

"You'll *need* it." Darlene narrowed her gaze.

"Your little squad only has six girls. Everyone knows it's the larger squads—like ours—that win. We can do awesome lifts and stunts."

"It's quality, not quantity that counts," Tabby insisted.

Wendi gave a vigorous nod. "Maybe we're small, but we have huge talent."

"Then how come you couldn't cheer the basketball team on to victory?" Kayla taunted.

"That's telling them, Kayla," Darlene said, laughing. "Although, I almost feel sorry for the Cheer Squad. I mean, how can they hope to succeed with a loser for a squad leader?"

Tabby saw pain flare in Wendi's gray eyes. Tabby tightened her hands into fists and raged at Darlene, "Wendi is *not* a loser—you are! Your father could spend zillions of dollars, but he can't buy talent for a no-talent like you."

"Of all the—!" Darlene sputtered in outrage.

Tabby turned swiftly to Wendi. "Let's leave before I do something with my food tray that I might regret."

"Thanks," Wendi said quietly as Tabby lead her toward their own table. "But I'm okay. I know they're wrong. Just because our squad is small doesn't mean we can't win."

"Absolutely. Talent, team spirit, and hard work matter more than a big squad and wealthy sponsor." Tabby flashed Wendi an encouraging smile. "And in two weeks, I predict we'll have a first-place trophy to prove it."

●●●●●●●●●●●

Four

"Open up!" Tabby cried in frustration as she pounded on the narrow metal door. She yanked hard on her combination lock, but her locker remained stuck.

"Come on, you stupid contraption! I'm already running late for practice. I need my duffle bag! OPEN!"

Still the lock didn't release. It had never given her trouble before—what was wrong with it?

Tabby checked to make sure she was in the right place. Locker number 31. The same one she'd used since September. And the lock didn't look different either—it just wouldn't budge.

Tabby took a deep breath and tried her combination again. The black dial spun from right to left to right. There was a soft click and the lock slipped open.

"YES!" Tabby said joyously, reaching inside for her duffle bag. Then she glanced at her watch and groaned. Cheerleading practice started five minutes ago.

Slamming her locker and snapping her lock in place, she turned and practically flew to the gym.

"Sorry I'm late," Tabby called out as she breezed into the large room. She smiled at Coach Laing and her four squad mates. *Four?* Someone was missing. She'd expected to be the last to arrive, but she wasn't.

Tabby asked curiously, "Where's Celine?"

"I have no idea." Coach Laing checked her watch. "But she better show soon."

"I'm sure she will," Wendi said, holding a notebook. "Celine is usually on time. And she knows this is an important practice. We have to work on the regional routine."

"I think we should include some of the Superstar moves," Coach Laing suggested. "That formation looked great."

"We also have to put in stunts. A basket toss or pyramid would impress the judges," Krystal said, looking up from the wooden floor, where she was stretching her legs.

"We'll definitely include stunts," Coach Laing assured her.

"I know we can't do a lot in two and a half minutes," Wendi said. "But there's a real awesome rotating lift that might be fun to try. I also have some other ideas to share."

Tabby nodded. She had already heard Wendi's ideas and thought they were fantastic.

"While we're waiting for Celine, I'll change into my sneakers," Tabby said, swinging her duffle bag by the strap as she walked to a folding chair.

But before she could sit down, the gym door burst open and Celine rushed in. Her short hair shone like black fire under the overhead lights and her face radiated excitement. "I just found out the most incredible news!"

Tabby, the other cheerleaders, and Coach Laing rushed over to Celine.

"What is it?" Krystal asked eagerly. "Did you win a zillion dollars, get discovered by a Hollywood agent, or fall madly in love with a hunky guy?"

"None of the above," Celine said with a wave of her hand. "Nothing that thrilling."

"Did your mother wake up from her coma?" Tabby asked in a more serious tone.

"Not yet." Celine shook her head. "Although the doctor thinks it will happen soon. But this is something totally different. I just found out that Sherry Bauer—"

"Who's that?" Krystal interrupted.

"The squad captain from my sixth-grade cheerleading group from San Jose. Only now she's the squad captain for Wilder Middle School. Anyway, Sherry's squad is going to be competing at the regionals, too. Can you believe it? I'll be competing against my own squad!"

"They're not your squad," Wendi reminded her. "We are."

Anna smiled at Celine. "It'll be fun for you to see your friends again."

"Yeah. It will. I think it will." Celine's black eyes grew thoughtful and she shifted uncertainly in her purple sneakers. "At least, I hope so."

"Enough chitchat." Coach Laing clapped her hands. "Okay, girls. Gossip session over. Let's get to work."

"Just a sec," Tabby said, hurrying back to the chair. "I have to change my shoes."

Tabby bent down and unzipped her duffle bag. Since money was tight at her home, she could only afford two pairs of cheer shoes: a comfortable pair for practice and the new pair for the regionals. The new uniform, gold poms, and shoes were neatly in her bedroom closet; her duffle bag held only practice clothes.

The other girls were already taking their positions in two lines, so Tabby hastily reached into the bag. But when her fingers touched one of her shoes, she heard an odd sloshing sound and felt something hard and wet.

When Tabby withdrew her hand, she stared in horror.

Her fingers dripped with a bright red liquid that looked just like blood!

●●●●●●●●●●

Five

"Tabby!" Wendi cried, hurrying over. "What's wrong?"

"My hand! Look!" Tabby held out her hand, feeling queasy. "Did I cut myself and not realize it? But it doesn't hurt."

Anna shook her dark head as she stood beside Tabby. "It doesn't hurt because that isn't blood. With two little brothers, I know cuts and scrapes when I see them. That looks like tomato juice."

Tabby lifted her hand to her nose and sniffed. Not tomatoes, but something sweet. Her shock shifted to curiosity and she reached into her duffle bag and carefully pulled out her shoe. A thin puddle of bright red liquid covered the inside of sneaker. And in the center of the puddle was a small square box—a familiar-looking carton.

"Plum Berry Punch!" Tabby exclaimed.

Coach Laing, Rachel, and Krystal had joined the circle around Tabby. Krystal squealed, "Ooh! What a gross mess!"

"You should know better than to leave a carton of fruit juice in with your clothes," Coach Laing said reproachfully.

"But I didn't do it!" Tabby protested, carefully holding the soggy sneaker in front of her. "Someone else put in here."

"Are you sure?" Coach Laing asked skeptically.

"Absolutely," Tabby insisted. "I didn't even bring a sack lunch today. I bought a hot lunch."

"You mean someone did this on purpose?" Anna's dark eyes opened wide with astonishment. "How could anyone be so mean?"

"I don't know. But look at my shoe! It's a drenched mess. At least I found the carton before it leaked on the rest of my stuff." Tabby licked a drop of plum juice as it dribbled down her wrist. Someone was out to get her. But who and why?

Tabby gave a heavy sigh. "You guys go ahead and start practicing without me. I better clean up." Then she headed for the restroom.

After tossing the sticky carton in the garbage, Tabby rinsed out her shoe and washed her hands. Tabby sadly gazed at her sneaker. Tonight she would bleach it white, but now it was a soggy, red mess. And there was no way she could wear it today.

So Tabby had to practice cheers in her bare feet. This worked out okay—almost. Once when Tabby tried a lift to Wendi's shoulders, Wendi's fingers brushed against Tabby's toes and tickled. Tabby giggled, lost her balance, and had to jump to the floor.

Everyone laughed, except Tabby, who blushed from embarrassment. She wasn't used to making mistakes—and she didn't like it one bit.

Tabby was relieved when practice ended.

"What a day!" Tabby exclaimed to Wendi as they gathered their belongings. "It took three tries before we managed to complete the rotating lift. It was hard to concentrate on locking my legs. I was too rattled about that dumb carton."

"I don't blame you." Wendi slipped her warm-up jacket on. "I wonder who put it in your shoe."

"I keep wondering, too. My duffle bag was in my locker all during school."

"Who knows your combination?"

"Only you and me." Tabby bit her lower lip. "Although, I *did* have trouble opening my lock before I came here—like it was jammed. Do you think someone tampered with it?"

"I bet that's it." Wendi pursed her lips and slowed her pace as they headed out of the gym. "Someone must have broken into your locker and put the Plum Berry Punch inside."

"But why in *my* shoe? It doesn't make any sense."

"It's a real puzzle." Wendi slung her backpack over her shoulder. "You're the one who reads all those mystery books. You should be able to figure it out."

"Yeah. You've got a point." Tabby felt a sudden rush of excitement. "I have to put my emotions aside and logically examine the evidence. Exhibit A: my jammed lock. Exhibit B: a leaky juice carton. And exhibit C: my sticky sneaker."

"Who do we know who brings Berry Punch cartons to school?" Wendi asked in a practical tone.

Tabby closed her eyes and thought hard. With her near-perfect memory, she could recall even the tiniest details. When she opened her eyes, she said, "I've seen Anna, Esteban, Celine, a Castle Hill cheerleader, and even my science teacher with that brand of fruit juice. It's really popular. I even have some at home."

"Me, too. Only I prefer Grape Berry Punch. It must have been someone with a grudge against you. Or maybe—" Wendi paused, looking excited—"maybe someone with a grudge against the entire Cheer Squad."

"Like Darlene Dittman!" Tabby guessed.

Wendi nodded. "This wouldn't be the first time Darlene's played a rotten trick on us. Remember the ruined sign-up sheet?"

"I'll never forget it. We were so discouraged. I thought we'd never become cheerleaders."

Wendi paused by the gym door. "Darlene never admitted it, but I know she was the one who sabotaged the sign-up sheet."

"Or her buddy LaShaun," Tabby suggested.

"Could be," Wendi replied. "LaShaun used to be nice. But now she dresses, talks, and even styles her hair like Darlene. It's like she's lost her own personality."

"And she'd do anything to impress Darlene." Tabby stood still, thinking back to this afternoon. Then suddenly she grabbed Wendi's hands. "When we stopped by the Castle Hill cheerleader table at lunch, LaShaun was drinking Plum Berry Punch."

"She was!" Wendi's gray eyes sparkled with interest. "So LaShaun or Darlene must have broken into your locker and dumped the carton in your shoe. This is all beginning to make sense."

"Yeah. Darlene was furious when I called her

a no-talent. This must be her way of getting revenge."

"The jerk!" Wendi clenched her fists. "I don't mind if she insults me—but this is too much!"

"I'm just glad the juice didn't ooze out of the shoe and ruin my clothes. That would have been a disaster. Luckily, little harm was done. I can clean my shoe at home."

"You're always so logical about everything," Wendi said with admiration. "I'm still ticked at Darlene. I want her to pay for pulling a nasty prank on you. We should report her to the principal."

"Not without proof," Tabby said, relieved to have figured out the sabotage mystery—and yet disappointed that the solution was so obvious. LaShaun *had* the juice carton. Darlene had a motive of revenge. End of mystery.

Still, Tabby knew a good detective must always keep an open mind. So Tabby told Wendi to wait a minute, then she hurried back into the restroom. Using a paper towel to protect herself, she plucked the sticky juice carton from the garbage.

When Tabby returned, Wendi raised her brows in surprise. "Why are you saving that gross carton?"

"For evidence." Tabby carefully zipped it in a side pouch on her backpack.

"Are you going to dust it for fingerprints, Sherlock?" Wendi asked with a teasing grin. "Or do you think LaShaun signed her name on the carton?"

Tabby grinned, not bothering to answer. It didn't make any sense to keep the carton. It was just an ordinary Plum Berry Punch container.

There was no telltale signature on it and she had no equipment for removing fingerprints. In truth, Tabby had no idea why she wanted the carton ... except for the strange feeling she might need it later.

●●●●●●●●●●●

Six

Saturday afternoon, Tabby stared into her closet anxiously. Her father would be here soon to take her to the parents' booster meeting at Wendi's house, and Tabby couldn't decide what to wear: her Cheer Squad T-shirt and green skirt? A comfortable pair of shorts and a sweatshirt? Or something more formal like a dress?

Finally, she settled on a denim jumper and a cotton-flowered shirt. It was semiformal and ultra comfortable.

Then Tabby grabbed a book and headed for the living room. Sitting in a blue recliner, she waited for the doorbell to ring.

I hope Dad isn't late, Tabby thought, glancing at the book in her hands. She giggled when she realized she had grabbed a dictionary instead of a mystery novel. *Gosh, I'm so flustered I'm not thinking straight. If I'm this anxious about a simple booster club meeting with my father, I'll probably really be a basket case when I actually go out on a date someday.*

"Figures a brainiac like you would read the dictionary," Adam said as he breezed into the living room, zapped on a sports channel, and plopped himself on the couch.

"I'm not ... I mean ... I was just waiting." Tabby tossed the dictionary aside and smoothed back her hair.

"Waiting for Dad?" Adam asked with a frown.

"Yeah." Tabby nodded. "Today's our booster-club meeting."

"Maybe Dad will show—but then maybe he won't," Adam warned. "He's a busy coach with better things to do than hang out with a bunch of girls."

"Dad cares about our booster club. Most of the parents will be there."

"Not Mom," Adam pointed out. "She has to work—too hard and too often."

"That's for sure. But luckily, Dad will be at my booster meeting," Tabby said confidently. Then the phone rang and all her confidence vanished. She clutched the chair arms anxiously. Was her father calling to cancel?

Of course, it isn't Dad, Tabby assured herself, letting the phone ring a second time and not moving to answer it.

"Aren't you going to get the danged phone?" Adam asked.

"No. I—I just can't. " Tabby shook her head. "You do it."

Adam groaned, but rose and grabbed the phone on the fourth ring. Tabby tensed and listened.

"Oh, it's you," Adam greeted in a bored tone.

"Who?" Tabby called out anxiously.

But Adam ignored her. "Yeah, it's me," Adam told the caller. "What's going down?"

That didn't sound like the way Adam spoke to their father, but still Tabby was unsure. "Adam, is that Dad?"

Adam put his hand over the receiver and said sharply, "Tabby, keep it quiet. I can't hear what Jake's saying."

Jake. Adam's closest friend.

Relief spread through Tabby like warm sunshine. And when the doorbell rang a few minutes later, Tabby raced to answer it. *I just know it's Dad. Mom and Adam are wrong about him. Dad wouldn't break his promise.*

And when Tabby opened the door, she wasn't disappointed. "Dad!" she exclaimed happily.

"Up close and in person." Mr. Greene stepped forward and hugged his daughter. "Looks like you're ready."

"Am I ever!"

"So come on," he said, taking her hand. "Let's make tracks to your booster club."

The Holcroft family room was filled with Cheer Squad girls and parents. Wendi's sister Valerie served coffee and iced tea, looking as gorgeous as always with her red-gold hair, slim figure, and wide charismatic smile.

Tabby waited until her father sat down, then she went over and whispered to Wendi, "This is like history in the making. The Cheer Squad's first booster club meeting!"

"It's great so many parents came," Wendi said, leaning against a wall and looking around the room. "Too bad Coach Laing couldn't come, too."

"She couldn't miss her own brother's wedding," Tabby said. "But she promised to make it to the next meeting."

"At least your father made it. I was kind of worried . . . I mean . . . I used to think he was a creep for spending so much time with your brother and ignoring you."

"He's not a creep—he is wonderful." Tabby grinned, her gaze settling on her father. He was deep in conversation with Wendi's mother. "And guess what he told me on the drive here?"

"What?" Wendi asked, pushing back her auburn bangs and leaning forward with interest.

"He broke up with Brenda."

"That skinny redhead with big ears?"

"Yes. She was too young for Dad, anyway. And she used to wear so much perfume, I could smell it on Adam when he came back from Dad's house."

"So does your Dad have a new girlfriend yet?"

"No—and I hope he never does," Tabby said firmly. Then she chuckled. "It looks like Dad's telling your mom his football stories. He's moving his hands like he's describing a touchdown."

"Mom loves talking sports. She was a star player on her college volleyball team and a football cheerleader."

"*Everyone* in your family was a cheerleader," Tabby teased. "Except maybe your father."

"Dad always said he would have been a cheerleader if he had better legs." Wendi giggled. "So he played soccer and now he coaches Little League. Being a sports nut is family tradition at the Holcroft house."

"Maybe I'll help make it a tradition in my family, too," Tabby said with a dreamy sigh. To herself she thought, *And hopefully my cheerleading will be the glue that bonds my family back together. Maybe both of my parents will come to the next booster club meeting.*

A short time later, Mrs. Holcroft stood before the other parents and thanked everyone for coming. Then she graciously introduced Mr. Greene and invited him to address the group.

Tabby beamed at the round of applause for her father. And when he began talking, she was proud of the way everyone listened with interest. He told a bit about himself; his years as a football player and his job as a college coach. Then he described the evolving sport of cheerleading.

"When I played ball in school, I didn't realize that cheerleaders were athletes, too. They were lovely gals and their chants made us guys feel important. But times have changed. At my college, the cheerleaders are highly respected. Many of them have earned scholarships through cheering."

"Valerie was offered a cheerleading scholarship," Mrs. Holcroft put in, gazing proudly at her eldest daughter.

"But I had to give up cheering to focus on my studies," Valerie said. "Still, the scholarship program is terrific."

"The girls can go a long way with cheerleading," Mr. Greene said as he pushed his wireframed glasses higher on his nose. "So I figure that as parents, we have a big responsibility. It's up to us to help our girls achieve their cheerleading dreams."

Tabby looked around the room at the other parents' faces. *They really respect my dad,* Tabby thought. *Even Rachel's parents who never approved of cheerleading seem interested. Celine's grandmother looks excited. And Krystal's father is actually taking notes!*

An hour later, Tabby's father had convinced everyone to help out with the regional competition. Wendi's sister and parents would coordinate transportation. Krystal's mother offered to help with music arrangement. Anna's Aunt Carlotta and Celine's grandmother would bring snacks and drinks. Rachel's father volunteered to videotape the competition.

"And I'll make sure the Cheer Squad's routine is topnotch," Mr. Greene declared, gesturing with his arms as he spoke. "I've rearranged my own schedule so I can attend some of the girls' practices. Coaching is what I do best."

Rachel's mother idly touched the pearls around her neck as she chuckled. "So you'll be the coach's coach."

"Excellent way of putting it." Mr. Greene looked flattered. "I'll do whatever I can to help the girls . . . especially my Tabby. There's nothing I wouldn't do for her."

Tabby felt such a burst of joy that she thought she might faint from happiness. *This has to be the best moment of my entire life,* she decided. *With Dad as our coach's coach, everything will be great. Nothing could possibly go wrong.*

Seven

After the booster-club meeting, Tabby made plans to sleep over at Wendi's house. The Holcrofts' home was alive with laughter and warmth, and Tabby loved being there. Tabby especially loved Wendi's cuddly marmalade cat Rufus, and often wished she could have a pet of her own. Unfortunately she lived in a no-pets-allowed apartment building.

After Tabby's father left, Tabby hugged Rufus to her chest and told Wendi, "What a great meeting!"

"The greatest." Wendi grinned.

"Yeah. Although, I'm glad it's over. Now we can hang out and talk or play games—just the two of us."

"Not exactly," Wendi said, clearing her throat and looking uneasy. "There's something I have to tell you. I invited someone else to stay the night, too."

"Who?" Tabby asked, expecting Wendi to say Rachel, Anna, or Krystal. Wrong! Tabby was totally blown away when Wendi said she'd invited Celine Jefferson. Celine had gone home, but she'd be back soon with her overnight bag.

"Why did you have to go invite *her?*" Tabby demanded. "Celine is so quiet and moody. I'm always afraid I'll say the wrong thing to her and she'll get mad."

"She's going through a tough time," Wendi explained, sitting on the living-room couch. "I guess I felt sorry for her. She looked lonely."

"I feel bad for her, too." Tabby sat beside Wendi. "But she has lots of friends at school. And she still has friends from her San Jose school. She doesn't act lonely."

"She's hiding her feelings with a tough attitude. And I thought being part of our sleepover might help us get to know her better." Wendi traced her fingers idly over the zigzag design on the couch pillow. "It'll be fun."

Later, Tabby was surprised to discover that Wendi was right. Celine, when she wasn't in a prickly mood, could be fun.

"Hey! Your bedroom has lots of space for tumbling!" Celine told Wendi as she dropped her overnight bag in the doorway and did a quick forward flip, landing gracefully on Wendi's bed.

Wendi giggled. "Now *that's* an entrance."

"Krystal would be jealous if she'd seen it," Tabby added, sitting in a chair by Wendi's computer. "Hi, Celine."

Wendi added, "Welcome to our mini sleepover."

"It was great of you to ask me." Celine fingercombed her silky black hair. "And I'm really wowed by your room." Wendi had her own computer, double closets, and a mirrored dresser. Celine pointed to Wendi's double bed and asked, "Do you ever jump on it like a trampoline?"

"Not since I was little." Wendi giggled. "Remember that silly chant about monkeys jumping on a bed? Well, my older sister used to tease me and say I'd fall off and break my head."

Tabby laughed, but she stopped when she saw a flash of pain cross Celine's face.

Celine must be thinking of her mother, Tabby guessed. I shouldn't have laughed.

But before Tabby could apologize, Celine's expression suddenly changed to joy. Celine jumped off the bed and grabbed a set of poms from Wendi's dresser.

"Let's practice cheers," Celine cried as she swished the poms. "How's this?"

> *Green and gold, green and gold,*
> *Knights forever, proud and bold!"*

On the word "bold" Celine slid into the splits.

"Smooth move," Wendi said, applauding.

"Maybe we can do it at the next basketball game," Tabby suggested.

"That'd be great." Celine stood up and grinned wickedly. "But do you have the courage to use the next verse?"

"Why wouldn't we?" Wendi asked.

"Listen, watch, and learn." Celine bent her arms, elbows out, poms on her waist. Then she lifted her head and kicked out.

> *Green and gold, green and gold,*
> *Knights forever, proud and bold!*
> *We're the top team, watch us score,*

We'll destroy our foes,
Till they cry, NO MORE!
We'll win the game,
Fair means or foul.
Gouge them in the eyeballs,
Kick them in the pants,
Then we'll do a victory dance!

"That's terrible!" Tabby doubled over with laughter. "I love it!"

"It's great in a really sick way!" Wendi laughed. "Too bad we can't use it."

"I didn't think we could," Celine said with a knowing smile. "When I cheered for the Matadors, we used to goof off with silly chants a lot. Not at games, of course. Sherry knew all kinds of funny chants."

"Was Sherry your best friend?" Tabby asked.

"The *very* best." Celine frowned. "But that was before my mom's accident. Everything's different now."

"You must miss Sherry and your other friends," Wendi said sympathetically.

"Sometimes. We had a great sixth-grade squad and we were planning to be even better in seventh grade." Celine sighed, then quickly added, "Of course, the Cheer Squad is pretty cool. I'm glad you invited me to join."

"We're glad, too." Tabby gave Celine a warm smile.

"At least you'll be able to see your San Jose friends in two weeks," Wendi added. "I'll bet you're excited."

"Excited isn't exactly the word. It'll be weird to compete against my friends . . . against Sherry."

Celine frowned, her hands strangling Wendi's poms. She was quiet for a moment, then suddenly her mood shifted, and she grinned. "Hey, isn't that our squad's scrapbook?"

Tabby followed Celine's gaze, recognizing the large rectangular book on the dresser.

"That's right." Wendi smiled. "The official Cheer Squad's scrapbook. Want to look at it?"

"Definitely!" Celine rang out.

"Me, too." Tabby knew how proud Wendi was of her scrapbook.

They sat on the carpet with the scrapbook in the middle. Wendi opened the book. "We have four pages filled with one newspaper article, several photos, and typed comments of mine."

"Four pages, already?" Celine said with awe. "Impressive."

"It'll be a while before we fill a scrapbook like my sister, but this is a start." Wendi flipped back a few pages and pointed at a newspaper article. "See, this is the article and picture from the Harvest Festival talent show."

Tabby smiled, thinking back on how much fun the contest had been. And getting their picture in the newspaper had been really exciting—like they were celebrities.

Wendi flipped to the next page. "Here we are at the homecoming rally."

Tabby giggled. While Tabby, Rachel, and Anna wore their usual green-and-gold skirts and T-shirts, Wendi, Celine, and Krystal wore goofy monster costumes. They had been advertising a haunted house fund-raiser that had been held at Anna's aunt's Victorian mansion. The event had been a "spook-tacular" success.

"The Cheer Squad has really come a long way—fast," Wendi said proudly. "A talent show, a fund-raiser, new uniforms, and in two weeks the regionals."

"The new routine is sure to wow the judges," Tabby said.

"It *is* good—better than the routines I used to do in San Jose." Celine smiled, but the smile didn't quite reach her eyes. "We might win first place."

"My father would really love that," Tabby added wistfully.

"Who wouldn't?" Wendi said, closing the scrapbook. "And we'll do our best—which is what's really important."

"Food, fun, and partying are important at sleepovers," Celine said, her ever-changing mood kicking in again. She stood up and swished Wendi's poms. "Got any good CDs? I can show you some hot dance steps. This is a slumber party, so let's party!"

For the next hour, Tabby felt as though she'd been swept up in a whirlwind named Celine. First they danced till they were giggling so hard they could barely breathe. Then they raided the fridge and snacked on the crazy combo of chocolate chip cookie dough, pickles, and cheese crackers. Afterward, they played a board game called Pick a Dream Date.

"Enough fun already!" Wendi declared, sinking onto her bed. "I'm bushed. Let's hit the sack."

"Me, too," Tabby said with an exhausted sigh.

"Wimps," Celine teased. But she yawned and admitted, "I guess it *is* late."

"Oh! I almost forget to type in my journal,"

Wendi said, going to her computer. She sat down, pushed a few buttons, and the screen glowed to life.

"Can't your journal wait till morning?" Tabby asked.

"I suppose so." Wendi covered a yawn with one hand. "But I have to at least check my E-mail."

"You get E-mail?" Celine asked, surprised.

"Sure." Wendi grinned. "I have a lot of friends on-line. It's kind of like having pen pals, but without the postage." She typed something in on her computer. "And yes! I have one message . . . but it doesn't say who it's from . . . that's odd."

"What?" Tabby questioned.

But Wendi didn't answer. And when Tabby turned to look at her friend, she saw that Wendi's mouth gaped open in astonishment and her face had turned pale.

"What is it?" Tabby asked, rushing over.

"The screen!" Wendi gasped and pointed. "LOOK!"

•••••••••••

Eight

Tabby stared in astonishment at the message on the computer screen: "DROP OUT OF THE REGIONALS—OR SUFFER!"

"This is a bad joke," Wendi said roughly.

"Who wrote it?" Tabby asked, her heart pounding rapidly. First plum juice in her shoe and now *this!*

"There's a coded e-mail address and phone number," Wendi said, her fingers flying and rows of numbers and symbols racing across the screen. "It was sent at one-fifty today."

"After the booster-club meeting," Tabby stated.

"But before I came over with my clothes," Celine added.

"I'll check the phone number and see who answers," Wendi said, reaching for her desk telephone and dialing. "Hello ... I received an E-mail message ... Oh, I see ... Thanks, anyway."

"Who was it?" Tabby asked eagerly.

"Pronto Print Shop." Wendi looked discouraged. "They make copies, sell stamps, send faxes and E-mail, and lots of other stuff. But they won't tell me who used one of their computers at 1:50. It's against their rules."

"Too bad," Celine said. "I guess we'll never know who the prankster is."

Wendi turned off her computer. "I wish I knew why someone sent that message."

"I'm more worried about *who*." Tabby frowned. "How far will he or she go to keep us out of the regionals?"

Celine shivered. "We could be in real danger."

"Well, I refuse to be scared off," Wendi said, striding over to her bed. "I'm not scared, I'm burning mad."

"I bet the lame person who sent this message also put the Plum Berry Punch in my sneaker," Tabby said.

"Do you think it was a Castle Hill cheerleader?" Celine asked anxiously.

"Probably." Wendi nodded. "Darlene wants her squad to be the only squad from Castle Hill Junior High at the competition. She's afraid we'll outdo her again. I guess she hopes we'll drop out or get so rattled we blow our routine."

"I *did* have trouble concentrating after finding the juice carton in my shoe," Tabby admitted.

"Knowing that someone is out to get us gives me a creepy feeling." Celine bit her lip. "What if the next prank is dangerous? Maybe we should forget the regionals."

"No way!" Tabby remembered the proud look in her father's eyes when he predicted the Cheer Squad would win first place. But there couldn't be a win if the squad didn't compete. And even worse—no competition meant no parents' booster club. Her father might lose interest in her.

Tabby lifted her chin with determination. "We *have* to compete."

"I feel the same way. I just hope there aren't any more pranks." Wendi rubbed her forehead wearily. "I don't want anyone to get hurt."

"No one will because I'm going to unmask the prankster," Tabby vowed. "Let's keep this warning a secret until I can find out who's responsible for the juice and E-mail."

"All right," Wendi said with a faint smile. "We're probably blowing this out of proportion anyway. Everything will be fine."

"How can we be sure?" Celine asked, clutching the bedspread with both hands. "You two have already been targeted. Doesn't it make you wonder?"

"Wonder what?" Tabby asked.

"Which Cheer Squad girl will be next," Celine answered grimly. "Anna, Krystal, Rachel . . ." Celine gulped. "Or *me*."

When Tabby returned home the following afternoon, she went straight to work. Her wish for a mystery had been answered, but now came the hard part—solving it.

To organize her thoughts, Tabby found a notebook and wrote at the top of a page, "Pranks."

But "Pranks" sounded so childish. Whoever tried to scare the Cheer Squad was serious. The juice could have destroyed Tabby's duffle bag and all its contents. And the E-mail was a bold, nasty threat. These were more than kindergarten pranks—they were *sabotage*.

Liking this word better, Tabby replaced "Pranks" on her paper and wrote "Sabotage." Then she turned to the next page and made another heading: "Suspects."

Think logically, she urged herself. *List every possible suspect.*

Darlene's name was number one on the list. Then LaShaun and the rest of the Castle Hill cheerleaders. Tabby even included Mr. Dittman, Darlene's father and squad coach.

Then just to be fair, Tabby listed her Cheer Squad teammates. They all had access to her duffle bag. Wendi even knew her locker combination. Of course, Tabby didn't really suspect her friends, but it made her list seem more professional.

My next step is to establish motive and opportunity for all of the suspects, Tabby mused. *No motive for the Cheer Squad. Everyone is eager to perform at the regionals.*

Realizing this fact made Tabby feel relieved. So she focused her attention on the prime suspect: Darlene Dittman.

Darlene has plenty of motive. She's probably heard that our new routine is terrific and she's afraid we'll do better than her squad. She's just sneaky enough to resort to low-life tricks.

"Checking out all the suspects would be a waste of time," Tabby muttered as she suddenly slapped her notebook shut. "Darlene Dittman *has* to be the saboteur. I just know it. But how can we prove it before she strikes again?"

"Kick higher, Tabby," Coach Laing ordered as she paced before the two lines of cheerleaders Monday afternoon.

"I'm trying," Tabby said, taking a deep breath.

"So try harder. Focus all your energy on your movements." Coach Laing stood before Tabby. "I get the feeling your mind is somewhere else. Are you still upset over that shoe trouble?"

"No . . . honestly . . . I'm fine." Tabby felt her face turn crimson, knowing that everyone was looking at her—including her father, who watched quietly from the bleachers. Embarrassing!

"My kicks will be perfect from now on," Tabby promised.

"Let's hope so," her coach replied. "Keep your head up, smile, and kick in sync."

"I will."

"Excuse me," a familiar voice interrupted. Tabby turned and saw her father had joined them.

"Is there something I can do for you, Mr. Greene?" Coach Laing asked, pushing back her beaded braids as she tilted her head toward Tabby's father.

"Actually, there's something *I* can do for *you*," Mr. Greene said with a quick smile. "Got a sec?"

"Of course. What's on your mind?"

Mr. Greene's smile widened. "I have a great view from the bleachers. I can see things you can't. And I know what the problem is."

"Problem?" Coach Laing asked cautiously.

"You got it. See, you're all wrong about my girl's kicks."

"I'm wrong?" Rusty Laing's tone was polite but her dark eyes had narrowed.

"Hey, it's no biggie. We coaches have to learn from our mistakes. I could tell you stories . . ."

He patted the young coach on the shoulder. "But I'll save them for later. Right now, we gotta shake those bugs out of your routine."

"And you're just the person to exterminate them?" Coach Laing asked with a stiff smile.

"You betcha I am!" Mr. Greene threw back his head and laughed. "Now first you need to move Tabby to the front row. See, her kicks aren't so bad. But her legs can't reach as high as the tall blond girl she's beside."

"Krystal?" Coach Laing turned, her expression tensing. "You mean because of the height difference? Well, I guess that could be a problem. Hmmm. Tabby, would you mind trading positions with Rachel?"

Tabby nodded eagerly, feeling a wave of pride in her father.

By the end of practice, Tabby was so flattered by her father's attention that she couldn't stop smiling.

"You're sure in a good mood," Wendi said as both girls changed out of their warm-up clothes in the gym's restroom. "Too bad you're the only one."

"What are you talking about?" Tabby asked. "Today was the best practice ever."

"You're kidding, right?" Wendi untied her shoes and gave Tabby a sharp look. "Everyone was uptight—especially Coach Laing."

"Then it was a good thing my dad was there to help," Tabby said. "The Castle Hill Cheerleaders aren't the only squad with an athletic professional. We're lucky Dad is guiding us."

"Your father isn't *guiding*—he's pushing. A hard push that's sending Coach Laing over the edge. Didn't you notice her gritting her teeth and glaring at your father?"

"That's not true!" Tabby cried, feeling a rush of hurt. "Everyone was glad that Dad was there. His suggestions were all wonderful."

"No way! By putting you in the front line, Rachel—who hasn't had any gymnastic training like you—has to do a back flip into the splits. But since Rachel can't do this, Celine has to trade places with *her*."

"That's not so bad," Tabby said defensively.

"Except that it messes up the basket toss sequence because you're the flier. Only now you're in the base position, so Coach Laing and I have to rework the entire routine." Wendi flipped her auburn ponytail over her shoulder and groaned. "Lucky to have your father? I think not."

Tabby's head throbbed and her heart stung. How could Wendi, her own best friend, say such mean things? Tabby felt tears swell in her eyes, blurring her vision, clouding Wendi's features so it was like looking at a stranger.

Then suddenly Wendi reached out and squeezed Tabby's hand. "Oh, I'm sorry! I didn't mean to hurt you."

Tabby looked down at her sneakers, too upset to reply.

"Really, I'm sorry. I was out of line. Maybe, I'm just tired and stressed out because of the regionals."

"Well, you shouldn't take it out on Dad." Tabby sniffed. "He was just . . . just helping."

"I know. I'm sorry I complained about him. Your father is really a great guy."

"The greatest." Tabby wiped her eyes and managed a weak smile. "I couldn't stand for you to resent him."

"I don't," Wendi assured her, picking up her backpack. "If he's a superdad to you, he's okay with me. And his ideas will probably improve our squad."

"Definitely," Tabby said.

But as she followed Wendi out of the restroom, she felt a sense of unease. And Tabby hoped she would never have to choose between two of the most important people in her life: her father and her best friend.

Nine

The following morning, Tabby awoke feeling refreshed and eager for school. Before she had fallen asleep, she and Wendi had spent two hours talking on the phone and now Tabby had no doubts about their friendship.

Wendi even offered to help Tabby investigate Darlene Dittman. *We'll be like Sherlock and Watson,* Tabby thought with a smile as she brushed her hair and pulled it back with a yellow hair band. *Detective Tabitha and her loyal assistant Wendi. It has a nice ring.*

Giggling to herself, Tabby grabbed her backpack and hurried down to breakfast. She was pleased to find her mother standing before the stove, flipping pancakes. Adam was already dressed for school. He sat at the table, pouring syrup over a tall stack of pancakes.

We're almost like a perfect family, Tabby thought as she sat down at the table, *except that we're missing one person.*

It was an enjoyable breakfast. Adam was in a

good mood and told funny football and basketball stories. Like his father, Adam could make ordinary incidents sound exciting or humorous. And Tabby's mother didn't seem tired. In fact, she shared some promising news. She had applied for a new job at a resort-styled elderly care home.

"Cross your fingers for me, kids," Mrs. Greene said, sipping her orange juice. "If I get this job, I'll make more money and work a day shift. We'll be able to do more things together."

"That'd be great!" Tabby said, reaching out to give her mother's hand a squeeze.

"Way to go, Mom," Adam added.

"Does this mean you'll be able to attend more of my cheerleading events?" Tabby asked.

"You bet."

"The regionals are less than two weeks away— on a Saturday. Dad will be there. It'd be great if you could, too."

"All I can say is that I'll try."

"Hey, what about me?" Adam asked. "I've got a wrestling meet this Saturday and the Winter Bowl game the next. Mom, you'll come watch, won't you?"

"I probably won't have the new job *that* soon, but who knows? I'll do my best." Mrs. Greene gave a soft sigh. "Kids, I know things have been rough since the divorce."

"That's for sure," Adam said with a frown.

Tabby thought of the lonely nights waiting for her mother to come home. "It *has* been hard."

"Well, this job could make our lives easier." Mrs. Greene gazed into Adam's face and then Tabby's. "Things will get better—and that's a promise you can trust."

*   *   *

An hour later, Tabby pressed up against a hall-way wall and tried to look invisible. She leaned toward Wendi, her Watson, and whispered, "There's Darlene's locker."

"And here comes Darlene!" Wendi whispered back.

"Shhsh! We don't want her to hear us. The idea is to observe and listen to *her*."

Tabby tensed and stared ahead, remembering the last time she had spied on someone. It had been a few months ago, when the Cheer Squad was just getting started. They had needed an-other girl to complete the squad, but when they asked Celine, she refused and acted mysterious. So Tabby and Wendi had played detective and shadowed Celine. It had been exciting—espe-cially when they uncovered the truth. Tabby crossed her fingers and hoped that she'd be able to uncover the truth this time, too.

Wendi clutched Tabby's hand. "Darlene is opening her locker."

Tabby quickly pulled out a small pair of binoc-ulars that her grandmother used to take to the opera. Peering through them, Tabby focused on the lock. "She turned to the right, but I missed the number, and now to the left . . . she stopped on number twenty-four! And then back to the right . . . thirty-five or thirty-six."

"Maybe this is how she learned your combination."

"Could be," Tabby said thoughtfully.

"Oooh! Look how full her locker is!" Wendi ex-claimed in a hushed tone. "Is that a picture of Brad Pitt taped to the door?"

Tabby nodded. "There's also a picture of Mark Stillman in his football uniform."

"He's a real hunk—and an eighth-grader. I'm not surprised Darlene is hung up on him. I wonder if Mark feels the same way about her."

"Probably. Guys go for Darlene's fake sweetness and snow-white blond hair," Tabby said.

"Lucky her." Wendi gave an envious sigh.

Tabby knew Wendi yearned for a boyfriend, but Tabby wasn't ready for romance. She continued peering through the binoculars and reported, "Darlene's textbooks are stacked neatly in one pile and there are magazines in another, a fancy makeup case, a boom box, and a bunch of Krunch candy bars."

"Perfect Darlene is into junk food," Wendi said with a giggle. Then she pointed. "Hey! Here comes Mark Stillman now."

"And T.J. Leposky is with him." Tabby put down the binoculars and watched as the two football players strode over to Darlene.

Suddenly Wendi grabbed Tabby's arm. "Hide your spyglasses. Teacher coming!"

Tabby whirled around and shoved her binoculars into her backpack. "Just relax and act normal."

"What's normal?" Wendi asked uneasily.

"Just act like we're talking."

"But we *are* talking," Wendi said with a giggle.

A moment later, Tabby breathed a heady sigh once the teacher passed.

"She didn't even look at us," Wendi said in relief.

"Well, school doesn't start for fifteen minutes," Tabby said logically. "There's nothing weird about two girls talking in the hallway. Now, back to sleuthing."

Darlene had shut her locker and was deep in a conversation with Mark and T.J.

"I wish we could hear what they're saying," Tabby said. "This is so frustrating. Darlene looks really excited."

"Who wouldn't be standing next to Mark?" Wendi replied dreamily.

"Shhsh," Tabby cautioned. "Stay here. I'm going to get closer."

"Darlene will see you!"

"No. I'll keep my back to her and pretend I'm opening a locker."

Before Wendi could stop her, Tabby was carefully moving forward. Tabby held her backpack in front of her chest, using it as a shield to halfway cover her face. She tensed as she neared Darlene, but then relaxed when it was clear Darlene was too busy talking to notice anyone else.

". . . would you do it for me?" Darlene said to the guys.

"Why should we?" Mark asked, his athletic frame hunched over so his face was close to Darlene's.

Darlene flashed a flirtatious smile. "It would mean so much to me. It's important that the Castle Hill Cheerleaders look good. Won't you help us win?"

"I don't like it," T.J. grumbled, shifting his large-sized sneakers. "It's just not right."

"We gotta think of our reputations," Mark added as he ran his fingers through his wavy hair.

"If you help us out, you'll have terrific reps with all the Castle Hill girls."

Tabby rolled her eyes, thinking that Darlene's sugary tone was sweet enough to rot teeth. What exactly did she want the guys to do? Tabby continued to twirl an unknown person's lock, listening and watching while other kids hurried by.

T.J. frowned. "The guys might hassle us."

"No, they won't," Darlene assured him. "But okay, if you won't do it as a favor, consider it a job. I'll pay you."

Tabby could swear that Mark's blue eyes flashed dollar signs. "How much?" he asked.

"Twenty," Darlene offered.

"Make it twenty-five," countered Mark.

"Twenty-five *each,*" T.J. put in with a cocky grin.

"All right. It's a deal."

"You want muscle, we got it." Mark flexed his arms.

"Thanks!" Darlene reached into her jeans' pocket and withdrew a folded paper. "Here. This is a schedule of practices and instructions. Don't show it to anyone."

"No problem there," Mark said. "I'd be happy if none of the guys ever finds out."

"Yeah," T.J. agreed quickly. "It just doesn't feel right."

"But helping our squad win is very right." Darlene smiled. "Those wimpy little Cheer Squad girls won't know what hit them. And by the time they find out—it'll be too late."

Ten

"I still can't believe it," Tabby told her Cheer Squad friends during lunch. All six girls sat at a back cafeteria table, and not one person was smiling.

"Darlene is even more rotten than I realized," Krystal said, twisting the guitar-patterned tie she had worn around her neck.

"Nothing like this ever happened on my old squad," Celine said, looking up from her milk carton. "It's creepy wondering when, where, or who will be targeted."

"Nothing bad is going to happen," Wendi stated practically. "Darlene wouldn't go that far."

"She broke into a locker to put juice in Tabby's shoe and then sent a poisonous E-mail warning," Celine said with a shudder. "She only cares about getting her way. And she wants our squad *out* of the way."

"I hope she didn't hire Mark and T.J. to *really* hurt us," Anna asked anxiously.

"No way!" Krystal said with angry fire in her blue eyes. "They better not even try."

"But Mark and T.J. are so big and muscular."
Anna's hand shook as she opened a bag of chili-
cheese chips. "We'd all better watch our backs."

Tabby shivered, hoping that Anna was wrong.
*If only I knew what was in the instructions Dar-
lene gave Mark and T.J.,* Tabby thought. *Then I
could stop anything terrible from happening.*

"These pranks are turning us into basket
cases," Wendi said. "We can't just wait around
for Darlene or her friends to strike. We have to
take action."

"Action?" Tabby repeated with a skip of her
heart. "What should we do?"

"Tell Coach Laing."

"Tell her that we were spying on Darlene?"
Tabby asked in dismay. "We can't do that."

"It's the only solution." Wendi unwrapped a
tuna fish on wheat bread sandwich. "Worrying
will drive us crazy."

Anna twisted a curl of her black hair around
her finger and suggested, "I could ask Esteban to
warn T.J. and Mark to back off."

"Esteban would do anything for me . . . I mean,
us," Krystal said with a dreamy smile. "Esteban
is tall, strong, and really smart. Darlene's hired
goons wouldn't dare mess with him. And maybe
he could get some of the other basketball players
to help."

"Muscle against muscle equals war," Tabby
stated as if reciting a math equation. "We have
to play by the rules or we'll be just as bad as
Darlene."

"Which means telling Coach Laing," Wendi
insisted.

Tabby exchanged worried glances with her

teammates. Fear and uncertainly seemed to swirl around them like chilly arctic breezes. Tabby hated the idea of running to a teacher with their problems, but they really didn't have a choice. Besides, Tabby wanted to support Wendi, so after a long pause she gave a grim nod. Anna and Rachel nodded, too. Then Krystal. And finally Celine. The decision was unanimous.

After school, Tabby went with Wendi to Coach Laing's office. Together, they told their coach the entire story.

Tabby had expected Rusty Laing to take immediate action. But instead Coach Laing idly fluffed her auburn-streaked black bangs and gave the girls a skeptical look. "Are you sure about this?"

"Absolutely!" Tabby answered. "I heard Darlene plotting with the two football players."

"But you didn't actually hear Darlene threaten anyone?" Coach Laing persisted.

"Well . . . no." Tabby shrugged. "But why else would she hire Mark and T.J.?"

"Darlene wants our squad out of the competition and she's paying Mark and T.J. to do her dirty work," Wendi added, standing beside Tabby.

"The guys seemed really reluctant, like Darlene was asking them to do something awful," Tabby said.

Wendi clenched her hands together. "And Darlene said the Cheer Squad wouldn't know what hit them . . . Us! . . . until it was too late."

Tabby shuddered. She'd seen both boys in action on the football field, charging forward like rampaging bulls and trampling anyone who got in their way.

"You have to stop Darlene," Tabby said. "She's pulling some kind of dirty trick to help her squad do better than us at the regionals."

"You're only guessing. The conversation you heard could mean a number of things."

"Like what?" Wendi asked.

"Darlene could have hired the boys to help drive cheerleaders to the regionals. Or perhaps she paid them to support the girls by showing up at the competition. Or maybe Darlene's squad needs strong guys to carry heavy props or equipment."

"I—I don't think so . . ." Tabby stared at her coach, doubt creeping into her mind. Suddenly Tabby wasn't sure what she had overhead. Had she jumped to the wrong conclusion?

"This is really bizarre." Coach Laing sighed. "I don't even understand why you girls were spying on another student."

Tabby felt her cheeks burn. Spying was fun, but admitting to spying was embarrassing.

"I can't go to the principal or to Coach Dittman without solid facts," Coach Laing went on with a shake of her head that caused her colorful beaded braids to rattle. "I'm sorry, but without real proof, there's nothing I can do."

Discouragement hit Tabby like a heavy blow. They'd tried and they'd failed. Now there was nothing to do but wait for something to happen . . . something *bad*.

Tabby and Wendi went into the gym without saying a word. It was hard to get psyched for cheerleading. Tabby went through the motions of changing into her practice outfit, but her heart wasn't in it.

Moments later, Coach Laing entered the gym, appearing confident and calm. "Warm-up, girls!" Rusty Laing gave a shrill toot of her whistle. "Stretch out. Get moving!"

Tabby dropped beside Wendi, spread her legs on the mat, and did some toe touches. It felt good to stretch her muscles, the stress easing from her body.

There was a soft bang of a door shutting. Tabby lifted her head toward the front of the large room and saw a man was entering the gym.

Her father!

Tabby jumped up off the mat, hurried across the floor, and hugged him. "I'm so glad you're here!" she told him.

"Did you ever doubt me?" he teased.

Tabby shook her head firmly. *If she had doubted her father, she never would again.*

"I'd better finish warming up," Tabby said, squeezing his hand fondly.

"Go to it, honey. I've got some things to discuss with your coach, anyhow."

Tabby walked slowly toward the mats, her gaze fixed on her father. He strode over to Coach Laing and greeted her with a friendly grin.

"I've been working on some ideas," Tabby heard him tell her coach. Tabby purposely sat on the mat nearest to her coach.

"That's nice," Coach Laing said coolly. "You can tell me about them after practice."

"Not soon enough. Your choreography is good, but it can be better. I'm here to see that happens."

"Lucky us." Rusty Laing gave a thin, strained smile. "Excuse me. I have a squad to coach."

Then she faced the Cheer Squad and clapped her hands. "Positions, girls!"

Tabby hesitated, unsure whether to go in the front or back line. "Where should I be?" she asked.

Wendi stepped forward and answered, "I think Tabby should take her old place in the second row. Rachel is still learning gymnastics and isn't comfortable with a back flip. Tumbling moves are easier for Tabby."

"That's ridiculous," Mr. Greene declared, stepping forward. "Tabby belongs in the front row."

"I'm not so sure," Coach Laing said in a stiff tone.

"A coach *needs* to be sure about everything," Mr. Greene boomed. "Tabby stays. And Rachel should work harder on her back flips. Or change the step to something easier. Maybe a sidestep or a flashy twirl. Then Rachel can do that snazzy slide into splits. She *can* do the splits, can't she?"

"Of course, I can!" Rachel cried defensively.

"So it's settled," Mr. Greene declared.

And Tabby stayed in the front row.

Dad is so wonderful, Tabby thought. *But Coach Laing doesn't seem to appreciate him. She didn't even say thank you.*

Tabby focused her thoughts on the routine, counting the one-two-three rhythm in her head; tumbling, spinning, and pumping her arms as she shouted chants.

"Very good!" Coach Laing praised when the squad landed in the finale, flipping over on their backs with one leg bent and their arms outstretched—like fallen angels. This gave a dramatic flare to the ending, and Tabby especially loved this move. So she was surprised to see her father frowning.

"Not bad," Mr. Greene told Coach Laing. "You've got some great choreography going here. Still, great can become *greater*."

"Oh? And I suppose you'll tell me how to achieve this greatness," Coach Laing said with heavy sarcasm.

"Be glad to." Mr. Green grinned. "You can add some pizzazz by having one of the gals jump into a forward flip with a twist at the end."

"I suppose you mean Tabby?" Coach Laing asked, raising her dark brows ominously.

"Great choice! Tabby can solo and strut her stuff while the others lie on their backs. Real zing of a finish!"

"I don't think that's a good idea." Coach Laing put her hands on her hips and looked sternly up at Mr. Greene. "And I'd appreciate it if you'd let me do my job."

"Can't blame a guy for being helpful," he said gruffly. "Most amateurs would be grateful for professional advice. Excuse me if I figured wrong."

"You're excused." Coach Laing lifted her head, then whirled around to face the squad.

Tabby could tell her father was annoyed, especially when he strode over to the bleachers and sat down with his arms folded across his chest.

Coach Laing was rude to my father! Tabby thought, dumbfounded. *I can't believe it! She's usually so nice, but not to Dad. She doesn't appreciate him. How can my coach be so unfair?*

Tabby tried to concentrate on practice. *I'll show Dad that he isn't the only professional in the fam-*

ily. I'll cheer so well, he'll be really proud of me,
she thought.

The squad went through the routine one more
time. A spin was added before the rotating lift,
so Tabby was now in a better position to climb
on Krystal's and Rachel's shoulders.

The routine went smoothly, and Tabby felt she
had done a good job. When she looked in the
bleachers, she saw her father raising his hand in
a salute to her.

Coach Laing seemed pleased, too. "Terrific!
Girls, you're doing wonderfully." She flashed a
bright smile. "I think we're ready to practice
with music."

The six girls lifted their poms and cheered.

"At last!" Wendi cried, squeezing Tabby's hand.
"Wait till you hear what Coach Laing and I put
together—a musical sequence that includes jazz,
rock, and rap."

"Sounds great," Tabby replied, imagining how
the routine would work with music. Fantastic! Of
course, the music only accompanied the beginning. After that, the squad would rouse the audience with lively chants and loud claps. It was
amazing how much went into a two-and-a-half
minute routine.

"Just a moment, while I get the tape from my
office," Coach Laing told the squad.

Tabby bent forward and stretched her calf
muscles while she waited. She waved at her father, who still watched from the bleachers. She
was just about to go over and talk with him when
Coach Laing returned—and she didn't look
happy.

Coach Laing hurried to the front of the room and declared, "Something terrible has happened."

"What?" Tabby and her teammates asked in unison.

"Look at this!" Coach Laing held out her hand, displaying a shredded dark mess. "The prankster has struck again."

Eleven

"What is it?" Tabby asked, staring at the confetti-like blob in Coach Laing's hand.

Coach Laing took a deep breath before answering, "It *used* to be our routine music. But someone pulled it apart—the tape is ruined."

"How could it happen?" Anna asked with disbelief.

"I have no idea," Coach Laing said, dark ribbons of tape draped over her fingers. "I listened to the tape yesterday at my apartment and it was fine."

"Could someone have gotten to it at your home?" Tabby asked, slipping into her detective mode.

"No. I wasn't even at home last night. My niece turned six and had a big birthday party, so I stayed overnight with them—and the tape was safely in a zipped compartment of my purse the entire time. Then this morning I came directly to school."

Tabby jotted down these facts in her mental

notebook. Then she questioned, "Where do you keep your purse at school?"

"In my office."

"Is your office locked?" Tabby asked.

Coach Laing nodded. "Whenever I'm giving a class, I lock the door. No one has a key, except for the principal."

"I know!" Krystal said with a theatrical toss of her blond head. "Principal Raymer did it!"

Celine and Anna giggled, but Coach Laing gave Krystal an "I-am-not-amused" look.

Tabby caught movement out of the corner of her eye, turned, and saw that her father had joined them. He faced Coach Laing and demanded, "Why the holdup? What's going on?"

"Nothing that concerns you," Rusty Laing said briskly.

Tabby quickly stepped between her coach and her father. "Dad, someone destroyed our competition tape."

"Why in the blazes would anyone do that?" Mr. Greene furrowed his brow and fixed an accusing gaze on Coach Laing. "How could you let something like this happen?"

"I didn't let it happen. It just did," Coach Laing snapped. "And I'll deal with it. It'll be a pain making another tape, but I'll do it tonight. Then the girls can use the music at our next practice."

"What about today?" Wendi asked. "We have fifteen minutes left."

"Let's just call it quits." Coach Laing gave a weary sigh. "Cool down, girls, and we'll meet tomorrow at Castle Mansion."

Tabby nodded. Anna's aunt, Carlotta Castle, was the Cheer Squad's advisor. Since the squad couldn't use the gym on Wednesdays, they met in Mrs. Castle's large basement dance studio, which was always fun.

Tabby followed Wendi back to the mats for some easy stretches. Afterward, they headed for the restroom so Tabby could change her clothes. Wendi only had to change her shoes, but Tabby could tell her friend was eager to talk alone.

"So what do you think?" Wendi asked as the door closed behind them.

"About what?" Tabby bent down to untie her shoes. Half of her mind was thinking about tomorrow's practice and wondering if her father would attend. She hoped so.

"Earth to Tabby," Wendi teased. "You're the one who's dying to solve the sabotage mystery. I figured you'd be bursting with ideas about the ruined tape."

"Oh . . . the tape. Too bad it was destroyed. I wonder how Darlene—or whoever—broke into Coach Laing's office."

"Maybe they swiped the keys," Wendi suggested.

"Maybe." Tabby glanced at her watch, seconds ticking by into minutes. "Can we talk about it later? I'm afraid Dad will leave before I can say good-bye."

"Sure. We can talk while we walk home." Wendi slipped into her brown loafers.

"Fine."

"Why don't you come to my house? We can have a sleuth session in my room."

"Sounds great!" Tabby's watch seemed to speed up. "First I gotta talk to Dad."

"I'll wait," Wendi promised as they left the restroom.

Tabby was relieved to spot her father still sitting in the bleachers. Even though most of the Cheer Squad had left, her father remained. *He must want to say good-bye to me,* she thought happily. *He really cares.*

"Dad!" Tabby called, hurrying forward with her duffle bag in one hand.

"There's my favorite athlete," he said, giving a light tug on her ponytail.

"I'm glad you're still here. It was great having you watch."

"Wild horses couldn't keep me from my favorite cheerleader."

"Does that mean you'll come tomorrow?" she asked hopefully.

"Tomorrow?" He pursed his lips as if thinking for a moment. "Sorry. No can do. I have another commitment."

"Oh." Tabby tried not to feel disappointed. "I understand."

"Hey, wipe off that frown. Wednesday may be out, but if I can juggle my schedule, I can probably swing Thursday. Okay?"

"Terrific! I'll see you then." Tabby glanced over at Wendi, who waited by the door. "Well, I better go."

"That's right." He took her hand. "With *me*."

"What do you mean?"

"I've already called and left a message on the machine for your mother." He flashed a huge grin. "Got a big surprise, Tabby-kitten."

"What?"

"It's father-daughter combo night. We'll go out for an early dinner and then an adventure of your choice—ice skating, a movie, or miniature golf. You name it—we'll do it."

Tabby's jaw dropped. "You mean it?"

"You bet," he boomed. "There isn't anything I'd rather do than be with you."

"Wow! That'd be terrific! But I don't know if Mom will approve. It's a school night and I have homework and chores . . ."

"I'll get you home in plenty of time to finish your homework. Besides, I'm your parent, too. And I say let's have some fun."

"Maybe we should invite Adam. I usually cook dinner when Mom works late."

"This is *our* night out. Adam won't mind," Mr. Greene said, giving Tabby's hand a warm squeeze. "He's a smart kid. He knows how to defrost a TV dinner."

"I guess so." Tabby was warmed by the genuine affection in her father's gaze. *I can't turn him down,* she decided. *Besides, I want to go more than anything.*

"Okay, Dad!" she declared with enthusiasm. "What are we waiting for? Let's jam out of here."

As they headed for the door, Tabby paused to talk to Wendi. "Change of plans. Dad's taking me out for dinner and an adventure."

"An adventure?" Wendi replied, surprised. "Now?"

"Yeah." Tabby grinned. "Isn't it great?"

"But what about our sleuthing session?"

"We can do that any time. I'll call you when I get home!"

Then Tabby gave a cheerful wave and left the gym, hand in hand with her father.

Twelve

Tabby tossed restlessly in her bed that night. She felt too full of confusing emotions to sleep.

I need to talk to someone, she thought. *But it's too late to call Wendi. If only I had gotten home early enough to return her phone call. But Dad kept me out until eleven—an hour past my bedtime. Darn! Wendi is probably mad at me, too.*

How could a terrific evening suddenly turn so terrible? Tabby had been having too much fun to notice the time—until it was too late.

And now everything is a mess, Tabby agonized.

Too bad she didn't have a computer journal to write in like Wendi. Then she could put her emotions into words and maybe lift some of the pain from her heart. But her memory served her so well, she didn't need a journal. Still, tonight was different. Ideas, feelings, and thoughts overwhelmed her. Maybe she could express herself by writing—not a journal, but a letter to a friend.

She reached for her backpack, pulled out her

notebook and a pen, then let her thoughts flow through her fingertips.

Dear Wendi,

I just had the most wonderful and terrible evening of my life. Being with Dad was the wonderful part. He has a gift for making people feel special. He told stories that made me laugh. He took me to this incredible Mongolian restaurant where they prepared the meat while we watched. The cook added anything we wanted—onions, pineapple, peppers, and more. Yummy! Dad made me feel grown up and important. After dinner, I remembered that Dad loved to bowl, so we ended up at Sierra Lanes. I've never bowled before, but I was willing to try. It was fun even though I was a DISASTER. I kept throwing the ball in the gutter. Dad didn't seem to mind. And he played a terrific game himself—scoring a 209. I was lucky to get 45. I had so much fun!

But then the terrible stuff happened after Dad dropped me at home. He didn't want to come in, which was probably a good idea. I thought Mom would be pleased I spent time with Dad. Wrong! She'd gotten off early and had planned a special dinner. How was I supposed to know? I can't read her mind.

Anyway, Mom chewed me out royally. She said I was becoming inconsiderate and irresponsible. She blamed it all on Dad. She said he was a bad influence—which is so wrong. And Adam made it worse by accusing me of taking Dad from him. It was a really ugly scene. And I felt so hurt.

Now I can't sleep and I'm really confused. I guess I was wrong to go with Dad without checking with Mom first. But Dad is my parent, too. How can spending an evening with him be bad?

The worst part is that now I know my parents won't get back together. Ever. Mom resents Dad, and Dad doesn't even mention Mom. I was just being silly hoping they'd fall in love again. I'll be lucky if they don't kill each other.

The sad truth is that happy endings don't happen much in real life. My family won't ever be a family again.

Tabby's fingers loosened and the pen fell from her fingers. A tear blotted the paper and another dribbled down her cheeks. Through blurry vision, she reread her own words.

I can't let anyone see this, she thought miserably. *Not even Wendi.*

Tabby ripped the letter from the notebook, crumpled it into a tight ball, and tossed it into the garbage.

Thirteen

"Why didn't you call last night?" Wendi turned from her locker to give Tabby a hard stare.

"Don't ask!" Tabby said wearily, dropping her duffle bag on the cement and spinning her lock until it clicked open.

"Are you okay?" Wendi pulled out two thick textbooks. "You aren't sick, are you?"

"Nothing like that. But my wonderful night with Dad caused a terrible argument with Mom."

"What a bummer. I knew you'd have a good reason for not calling. Tell me about it," Wendi said gently.

Tabby hesitated, afraid she'd cry again. She took a deep breath and poured out the whole story: the great time with her Dad, the blowup with her mother, and the continued cold shoulder from her mother this morning. No friendly "good morning," no pleasant breakfast talk, and no kiss good-bye. Her mother was steamed—for sure!

"I don't know what to do," Tabby said. "Mom has a right to be mad. I should have checked with her before leaving with Dad. But it's impossible to make them both happy."

"Divorce sucks," Wendi said with a sympathetic nod. "Still, you live with your mom so you should follow her rules."

"I usually do. Then the one time I do something wrong, Mom goes ballistic. It's not fair."

The warning bell rang.

"I'm sure your mom will forgive you. She's usually pretty cool." Wendi gave Tabby a faint smile. "I better go."

"Me, too." Tabby grabbed her books. "Thanks for listening. It helped."

"Any time," Wendi said warmly. "And at lunch we'll work on the sabotage mystery. That'll keep your mind off your parents."

"I hope so." Tabby hugged her books to her chest, sighed, then headed for her first class.

During break, Tabby didn't need to go to her locker, so she stopped by the girls' restroom to fix her hair. She brushed her honey-blond hair until it looked soft and shiny, then she tamed it with a blue scrunchie. Putting away her brush, she left the restroom.

As she turned the hall corner, she saw Mark Stillman and Darlene Dittman. They stood by a bank of lockers, their heads bent together as they talked softly.

They must be plotting against the Cheer Squad! Tabby realized.

Darlene suddenly looked up and gazed directly at Tabby.

Tabby stiffened, then quickly glanced down and pretended to adjust her backpack strap. Her hands shook and she almost dropped her backpack. *Act cool,* she warned herself.

Out of the corner of her eye, Tabby saw Darlene whisper something to Mark. Then Darlene pointed directly at Tabby. Mark shrugged and held out his hand. Darlene seemed nervous as she reached into her pocket and slapped something green on Mark's palm—money!

Payoff time, Tabby guessed, turning slowly and taking a few steps the opposite way down the hall.

When she paused and glanced over her shoulder, she saw that Darlene was leaving and Mark had pulled out his wallet. Yes! He was slipping the green bill in his wallet. It must be a twenty—a payoff for hired muscle or the reward for breaking into Coach Laing's office and destroying the tape?

The warning bell rang and Tabby saw Mark shove his wallet into his jeans pocket. When his hand came up, a small piece of white paper fluttered to the floor. Mark didn't seem to notice the paper as he hurried away.

Now's my chance! Tabby realized, running forward and scooping up the paper. Bursting with excitement, Tabby read its message:

5:00 shape-up wed #3

"Huh?" Tabby murmured to herself. "Shape-Up for *what?* And what is number three?" She shrugged. She didn't have time to figure it out now, so she carefully folded the paper, put it in a zipper pouch in her binder, then hurried to her next class.

Tabby was late to lunch because her class was planning a field trip and her teacher ran out of parent permission forms. After searching through several files, her teacher finally found a form for Tabby. Grabbing it, Tabby hurried to the cafeteria.

As she approached the back table where Anna, Krystal, and Wendi sat, her friends noticed her. They shared glances, then immediately stopped talking. Tabby had the uneasy sense that they'd been talking about *her*.

But when Wendi flashed a warm smile, Tabby told herself she was just being overimaginative. These were her friends. They would never talk behind her back.

Tabby sat beside Wendi, then showed everyone Mark's note.

"What's it mean?" Wendi asked, wrinkling her nose as she read the cryptic words.

"I thought 'wed' might mean wedding." Tabby poked a straw in her apple-juice carton and took a sip.

Krystal ripped open a bag of cheese popcorn. "Maybe Mark needs to shape up before the wedding."

"I'll volunteer to be the bride," Wendi teased.

Everyone laughed, except Tabby who suddenly jumped in her seat and snapped her fingers. "Shape-up! I should have realized it sooner!"

"What?" Wendi, Krystal, and Anna asked.

"Don't you recognize it? It's the name of that new gym—the one that's run by LaShaun Penner's family. Mark must be meeting Darlene there at five."

"On Wednesday!" Wendi exclaimed with shining gray eyes. " 'Wed' is short for Wednesday—today!"

Unwrapping a triple decker turkey sandwich, Anna raised her brows and wondered, "But what does '#3' mean?"

"I don't know," Tabby replied, tapping her fingers on the smooth table. "But I know how we can find out."

"How?" Wendi wanted to know.

Tabby grinned and patted her friend on the hand. "We'll find out after school. You and I are going to Shape-Up Gym."

After several miles of bike riding, Tabby and Wendi arrived at the modern, impressive gym at twenty minutes before five.

"I hope Darlene doesn't see us," Wendi said as she wove a chain through her bicycle spokes and fastened a lock.

"We'll have to be careful," Tabby said with a solemn expression. "Let's go inside and scope out the place."

Wendi bit her lip uneasily, but nodded.

Moments later, they entered a wide lobby with plush orange carpeting and unusual abstract statues and paintings. High star-shaped lights twinkled a greeting—or maybe a warning. A receptionist was talking on the phone and didn't seem to notice them.

"Which way do we go?" Tabby whispered to Wendi as they breezed past the receptionist.

"You choose. Right, left, or middle hallway."

Tabby pointed to a door with a number one painted in bright orange. "Remember the note had a '#3' on it. Maybe we should look for room number three."

"Good thinking. Then we'd better go down the left hallway."

Tabby held her breath when a group of young girls—probably third-graders—came out of room number two. They all wore pink tights and black ballet shoes. They were laughing and talking among themselves and didn't even glance at Tabby or Wendi.

The hallway suddenly reached a dead end.

"Room number three isn't here. Let's try the right hallway," Wendi suggested.

Tabby agreed, crossing her fingers and praying that they wouldn't bump into Darlene or Mark.

Some adults holding tiny children walked by and Tabby whispered, "Just pretend we belong here."

"I'm pretending," Wendi said with a forced smile.

They reached a hall intersection and cautiously looked around. More adults and little kids, but no sign of Darlene. And the receptionist was still on the phone. Thank goodness!

"Follow me," Tabby said, darting furtively across the hall.

"There's only one door and it's at the end," Wendi said, pointing. "Check out the number."

"Three," Tabby replied in a hushed tone. "And the door is open a crack. Come on, let's go look inside."

"I'm with you," Wendi said through clenched teeth.

Tabby took a deep breath and advanced forward. Her ears were perked for any strange noises.

She glanced behind a few times and was satisfied that no one was following them.

When they stood before door number 3, Wendi hesitated and told Tabby, "You look."

"All right." Tabby gulped and leaned forward. She put a hand on the wall for support and peered into the room. She saw gym equipment: floor mats, balance beams, and uneven bars.

"Is Darlene in there?" Wendi whispered.

"I don't see her . . . but I think I see her father," Tabby said excitedly. "A tall blond man."

"That sounds like Mr. Dittman—or as Krystal calls him, Mr. Toilet King."

Tabby giggled, but it sounded more like a squeak. She shifted her feet and tried to get a better view. "Mr. Toilet King is talking to someone."

"Is it Darlene?" Wendi asked.

"No . . . not a girl," Tabby replied in a hushed voice. "A man, I think, but he's standing behind a pile of mats."

"Maybe it's Mark!"

"He's not tall enough, but he's stocky."

"T.J.?"

Tabby shook her head, wishing the man would move so she could see his face.

A moment later, she got her wish. But when she saw the man's face, she nearly fainted.

It wasn't possible!

Totally, completely, impossible!

And yet there was no mistaking those broad shoulders, the sandy-brown hair, and the glasses.

But what in the world was Tabby's father doing *here?*

Fourteen

"Now will you tell me why we had to leave?" Wendi asked, slowing her bike to a stop before a shady park. "Who was that guy with Mr. Dittman?"

"I—I can't . . . I just don't believe it." Tabby clutched her handlebars tightly. Then she hung her head and spit out the words, "It was my father."

"No way! Your dad in the enemy's camp?"

"It was him all right," Tabby said miserably. "But I have no idea why he was there. It just doesn't make any sense."

"Maybe or maybe not," Wendi said cryptically, pursing her lips as if she was thinking deeply. "Let's go to my house. We really have to talk."

Tabby gave Wendi a puzzled glance. Wendi sounded so serious, as though she were about to reveal a terrible secret. And Tabby remembered how her friends had stopped talking when she had shown up at lunch today. Had they been talking about *her?*

A cold fear filled Tabby and she pedaled faster. She *had* to find out what was going on.

Usually Tabby looked for Rufus when she went to Wendi's house, but today she passed by the kitchen where Rufus usually lounged on the fridge and followed Wendi to her bedroom.

Once inside, Tabby sat on the edge of Wendi's bed and faced her friend. "Okay. Out with it."

"I don't know how to begin . . ." Wendi reached out and hugged a small heart-shaped pillow to her chest.

Tabby looked directly in Wendi's eyes. "Best friends don't keep secrets from each other."

"It's not exactly a secret. See, the other girls asked me to talk to you."

"About what?"

Wendi blew out the deep breath she had taken. "About . . . your . . . your father."

Tabby frowned. "What about him?"

"Well, everyone thinks the booster club was a great idea. But they don't like how he's butting in at practice. He's making Coach Laing nervous . . . and the rest of us, too."

"Does that include you?" Tabby demanded, her hands clenched in her lap.

Wendi hesitated, then nodded. "I know he means well," she said quickly. "He's being helpful, but he's too pushy. It would be better for everyone if he stopped coming to practice."

"Better for everyone except *me*." Tabby struggled to keep her voice calm. She usually prided herself on being cool, calm, and intelligent. Losing emotional control was okay for other people, but not her. And yet a sharp pain of betrayal stung her heart.

"Tabby, I understand how much your dad means to you. He's really great—when he's not trying to run our squad."

"Dad's just a take-charge guy. I've always been so envious of Adam for getting all Dad's attention—and now suddenly Dad is interested in me."

"I know how you feel," Wendi said sincerely. "But I am the squad captain. I have to consider what's best for the entire squad."

"What are you trying to say?"

"Please don't be mad, Tabby. I care about you and I'm thrilled your dad is hanging out with you. But he's making the rest of us miserable."

"That's not true! He's improving the squad."

"No, he isn't. He's interfering and making outrageous demands. Everyone is uncomfortable. That's why you have to tell him to stay away."

Tabby gasped—Wendi's words hit her like a slap in the face.

"Don't be upset," Wendi pleaded.

"Too late!" Tabby snapped.

Then she stood up swiftly, wiped a tear from her cheek, and ran out of the room, out of the Holcroft house, and maybe out of her best friend's life forever.

● ● ● ● ● ● ● ● ● ● ●

Fifteen

The phone rang, but Tabby didn't answer. The machine picked up after four rings and Tabby heard Wendi's voice leaving another message. That made five.

Wendi can leave all the messages she wants, but I still won't talk with her, Tabby thought stubbornly. *And I don't want to go to cheer practice tonight either. Those girls aren't my friends anymore. Real friends don't talk behind your back.*

Tabby dabbed her eyes with a tissue and leaned back in the recliner. For once she was glad to be alone in the apartment because no one was around to see her cry. If Adam were here, he'd probably tease her about her red nose and call her "Rudolph." And her mother would get all emotional, smother her with concern, and end up crying, too.

Suddenly, someone knocked at the front door.

Tabby tensed. *Was it Wendi?*

The knocking persisted and Tabby heard a deep voice call out her name.

"Dad!" Tabby hurried to the door and said, "What a surprise!" Of course, the biggest surprise had been seeing him with Mr. Dittman an hour ago, but Tabby didn't add that. She was sure there was a logical explanation for it . . . at least she hoped so.

Mr. Greene hesitated on the threshold and peered into the room. "Your mother isn't here, is she? I don't have time for a heavy scene with her."

"She's at work." Tabby gave a bittersweet smile. "So the coast is clear. You can come in."

"Great!" He pushed his glasses up on his nose and took a seat on the couch. "I've got something real important to discuss with you."

"What?" Tabby ran her fingers over the couch's arm nervously as she faced her father. She replayed Wendi's words in her mind and wondered if she should tell her father to stop coming to practice. *But I want him there!* Tabby thought, feeling angry at her friends all over again. *I can't tell him to stay away.*

"Honey," her father began, gently taking Tabby's hands in his own, "you look like you've been crying. And I know why."

"You do?"

"Of course. I've been worried about the same problem. You're on a sinking ship and I want to save you from drowning."

"Sinking ship?" Tabby blinked. "What do you mean?"

"The Cheer Squad is the Titanic—and that danged coach of yours is one big iceberg." He raked his fingers through his smooth sandy-brown hair. "Honey, you can achieve great things. You want to win at the regionals, don't ya?"

"Winning would be nice, but what's that—"

"I knew you wanted to be a winner," he said swiftly. "That's why I'm so darned frustrated. It's clear you won't win as long as you're on the Cheer Squad."

Tabby simply stared in astonishment.

"Coach Laing is holding you back," Mr. Greene went on. "You need a coach who will appreciate your talent. And I have the solution."

"Solution?" Tabby's head spun.

"You got it!" He flashed a grin. "Guess where I've just come from."

"Uh . . . Shape-Up Gym."

Now it was his turn to stare in surprise. Then he chuckled. "You *are* a smart cookie. Yup, that's where I was, talking to an old pal of mine, the King of Plumbing himself, Ronald Dittman. And guess what, honey?"

Tabby shook her head, afraid to speak, think, or guess.

"I solved your problem. You can say good-bye to Coach Laing and the Cheer Squad. Thanks to my old pal Ron, you're now a member of the Castle Hill Cheerleaders."

••••••••••

Sixteen

"I don't want to be a Castle Hill cheerleader!" Tabby told her father over and over. But he didn't seem to hear her—or chose not to. He just smiled confidently, ruffled her hair, and told her to think it over. Then he glanced at his watch and said he had to hurry back to his college.

When the door shut behind her father, once again Tabby was alone.

I can't believe my life! Tabby thought, pacing the living room and shaking her head. *My Cheer Squad friends don't want Dad at practice and now Dad doesn't want me there, either. Mom and Adam are probably still steamed at me, too. Everyone is pulling me in different directions, and I don't know which direction is the right one.*

She yanked a crocheted afghan off the back of the couch and wrapped it around her shoulders. Curling up in a corner of the couch, Tabby huddled within the brightly colored afghan. If only she could stay wrapped in a safe cocoon forever, but what would that solve?

Glancing at the digital time on the VCR, Tabby groaned. The Cheer Squad would be meeting at Castle Mansion in an hour.

What should I do? Tabby agonized. *I love the Cheer Squad. But how can I go there when I know everyone resents Dad? If they don't want Dad, they don't want me either.*

Tabby clutched the soft yarn and felt her heart breaking. She couldn't stay in the Cheer Squad—not now.

Maybe she *should* consider her father's solution—becoming a Castle Hill Cheerleader. Did that mean she'd start palling around with Darlene? Would she spend weekends at Darlene's fancy split-level house instead of Wendi's cozy home? Would she help Darlene plot more sabotage against the Cheer Squad?

"NEVER!" Tabby cried out, sitting up straight. "My friends may have hurt me, but I don't want to hurt them. Although, maybe I could find out if Darlene is planning any more mean pranks—if I joined the Castle Hill Cheerleaders."

Tabby pursed her lips and tried to imagine herself cheering beside Darlene, LaShaun, Kayla, and the other Castle Hill girls. Unthinkable! And yet it would be a way to solve the sabotage mystery. But was the price too high?

Tabby sighed, remembering how she'd once worried about having to choose between her father or Wendi. This is much worse, she thought. *I have to decide between Dad and the entire Cheer Squad.*

When her mother came home from work forty-five minutes later, Tabby had thought so hard her head ached. Making choices wasn't easy. But at last she had come to a decision—a very difficult decision—and she knew it was the right one.

Tabby could hear distant music as she walked up the steep steps. Her palms were clammy and she had the urge to turn around and hop back into her mother's car. But she refused to run from her problems. So she squared her shoulders and knocked on the ornate wooden door. Behind her, she heard her mother's car drive away.

No one answered the door, so Tabby knocked again.

"The Cheer Squad must be in the dungeon," Tabby told herself, referring to the basement dance studio. Krystal sometimes teased that when the room was dark, it was like a dungeon.

Tabby jiggled the doorknob. "Darn, it's locked. Now I'll have to go around the back."

Sighing, Tabby descended the steep steps and took a rough dirt pathway that crossed in front of the rambling mansion, around to a patio that was usually unlocked. Once she entered the patio, she could follow a steep staircase into the basement.

Lights from inside the house illuminated the overgrown yard. Tabby jumped off the path so she wouldn't trip over a rock, but she stumbled anyway and ended up stubbing her toe on a fallen oak branch.

"Ouch!" she muttered, leaning against an enormous tree trunk.

As she rubbed her throbbing toe, she heard a low rustling sound. Startled, she froze in place. Peering into the semidarkness, she saw movement in dense oleander bushes near a square basement window. She covered her mouth so she wouldn't cry out. Two people were crouched down and peering through the window—spying on the Cheer Squad practice!

Fear switched to anger when Tabby recognized the two figures—Darlene and LaShaun! Were they plotting more sabotage?

I've got to stop them, Tabby thought anxiously.

"What's that noise?" Darlene whispered loud enough for Tabby to hear.

"Maybe a cat or squirrel. It came from over there," LaShaun said in a quivering voice. Then she pointed directly to the tree that Tabby crouched beside.

Tabby felt trapped. She stood as still as the tree trunk, trying to blend in with nature. But then she asked herself, *Why am I hiding? I have every right to be here. It's Darlene and LaShaun who are trespassing.*

Before Tabby could come up with a solid plan, she boldly left the shadows and demanded, "What are you doing in Mrs. Castle's bushes?"

Darlene jumped up with a shriek.

"We're dead!" LaShaun clutched Darlene's arm and cried, "I'm outta here!"

"Wait a sec," Darlene ordered in a calm tone. "It's only Tabby—the girl dad said wanted to join our squad."

"Can't blame her for that," LaShaun said. "Anyone can see that we're the best squad at CHJH."

Tabby felt her cheeks flame. She put her hands on her hips and challenged, "So how come you're sneaking around here?"

"We got our reasons," Darlene replied mysteriously. "And we aren't telling you until we're sure you're with us."

"I'm not in there practicing, am I?" Tabby countered, pointing through the small window. Through it she could see Coach Laing spotting for Anna as the petite dark-haired girl was lifted to Krystal's and Rachel's shoulders. *Anna is doing my stunt. I should be the flier,* Tabby thought with a sharp pang.

"So how come you want to change squads?" Darlene demanded.

"It was my father's idea," Tabby answered truthfully. "He and Coach Laing don't get along."

"Well, your dad and mine are longtime friends. And my father is spending megabucks to make sure our squad wins first place at the regionals. You'd never catch our squad practicing in a drafty basement. We have state-of-the-art exercise equipment."

"My family owns Shape-Up Gym," LaShaun boasted.

"That's a really cool place—much cooler than the school gym or a basement." Tabby paused, her mind racing. More than anything she wanted to tell Darlene and LaShaun what they could do with their snobby squad. But solving the sabotage mystery was more important. What if Mark and T.J. were planning to seriously injure someone on the Cheer Squad? Tabby had to stop them.

"So why are *you* here?" Darlene's sharp gaze matched the edge in her words. "I thought you were through with the loser squad."

"They are not . . . I mean, well, I came to tell them I quit," Tabby lied. "Now it's your turn to tell me why you're here? Are you planning anything . . . uh . . . exciting?"

"Winning at regionals will be very exciting," Darlene said.

"Our routine is fantastic, but it doesn't hurt to check out the competition," LaShaun added.

Darlene tossed her white-blond head. "And from what I see, the Cheer Squad doesn't have a chance. What a pitiful stunt! Anna fell down twice."

That's because Anna is having to take my place, Tabby thought guiltily. But aloud she said, "Maybe they'll follow the prankster's advice and drop out of the regionals."

"Oh, I heard about those pranks," Darlene said, moving away from the window. "Bet your ex-squad pals were really freaked."

"For sure," Tabby replied. "Actually, I kind of admire the prankster. Breaking into my locker and Coach Laing's office took a lot of courage and brains."

"Brilliant and gutsy," Darlene said with a nod.

"I heard your shoe was major disgusting," LaShaun said, giggling. "Wish I could have been there to see the fireworks."

"It *was* kind of funny." Tabby forced a smile on her face and crossed her fingers behind her back. "I bet the next prank will be megacool. I'd love to help plot it. It'd be fun to watch my ex-friends freak out."

"Stand in line," Darlene said with a shrug. "But I haven't a clue who the prankster is."

"Don't con me," Tabby said with a sly smile. "I *know* you *know* who played those pranks. Come on . . . how did you do it?"

"We really don't know," LaShaun insisted, plucking a leaf out of her black hair. "But we're dying to find out."

Darlene nodded. "I've asked all kinds of kids and no one knows anything. It's weird. I'm beginning to think it's an inside job. Maybe you!" Darlene and LaShaun laughed. "*You* could have staged the locker break in and the E-mail warning."

"Funny." Tabby tried to laugh along with them. "But I don't know how to break into Coach Laing's office. Are you sure *you* didn't hire someone to do it . . . like Mark Stillman?"

"I figured you saw us together," Darlene said with a shrug. "But you won't see us together anymore. Oh, I hired Mark and T.J. all right. But not for pranks—for stunts."

"Mark and T.J. are both scummy dirtbags." LaShaun patted Darlene sympathetically on the arm. "We don't need them."

"I paid them to do a job and they backed out—and kept the money!" Darlene's pale face seem to flame like a lit match in the darkness. "So what if the other guys were ribbing them? We need their muscle on our squad. Now we'll have to drop out of the coed division—which means only competing in one division."

Tabby stared in amazement, realization sinking in. The Castle Hill Cheerleaders had entered in the coed division! That's why Darlene bribed Mark and T.J. They needed the boys for lifts and stunts. It had nothing to do with the Cheer Squad.

"You honestly don't know who's responsible for

the pranks," Tabby said, her shoulders slumping in discouragement.

"I don't have a clue." Darlene looked annoyed. "It's not like I care about the Cheer Squad's problems. Let's jam out of this creepy place. No wonder they had a haunted house here. Anyway, we don't need to check out the Cheer Squad's routine since you're with us. You can show us their best moves and we'll copy some to embarrass them. Only we'll make sure our routine is the *best*."

Tabby stared in shock at Darlene—not because of her low-down plan—but because Darlene genuinely seemed to know nothing about the saboteur. *I was so sure she was guilty,* Tabby thought in confusion.

Darlene was talking about how Tabby could double-cross the Cheer Squad *and* help her new squad mates with their homework. "We can really use a whiz kid like you on the squad. And your cheer moves aren't bad, either."

"No one is going to *use* me," Tabby snapped.

"What's with the attitude?" Darlene asked.

"The game's over. I'm not quitting the Cheer Squad. I'm not joining your squad. And no way am I ever going to ace your homework for you or anyone else!" Tabby raised her arm and pointed accusingly at the two surprised girls. "And you are trespassing on my friend's property. You don't belong here any more than I belong on your snooty squad. So get lost!"

Seventeen

Tabby was still shaking with anger when she walked into the dungeon minutes later.

"Tabby!" Wendi called out joyfully, rushing over to give her a hug. "I was afraid you weren't coming."

"I tried not to, but I couldn't stay away." Tabby smiled at Wendi, then her gaze swept across the room to Anna, Krystal, Celine, Rachel, and Coach Laing. *My real friends,* she thought in relief. *It feels right to be here.*

"I'm sorry for everything," Wendi said emotionally. "When you wouldn't answer the phone, I felt terrible. I can't stand for you to be mad at me."

"I'm not," Tabby assured her. "And now I have important news for the whole squad. You'll never guess who I just talked to."

Moments later, Tabby stood in front of her five squad mates and her coach. "First of all, I want to apologize to everyone because of my father."

"Tabby, you don't need to apologize," Coach Laing said gently. "I know your father was trying to be helpful. He got a little pushy, but I should have talked to him about it. There was no need to involve you."

Krystal gave Tabby a sorrowful look. "I'm sorry your feelings were hurt."

"I'm very, very, *very* sorry," Wendi added sincerely.

"It's okay," Tabby said, smiling. "I was so overwhelmed by Dad's attention that I didn't realize how you guys felt. Dad can be pushy. That's what makes him a good football coach—not a good cheerleading coach."

"If he wants to keep coming to practice," Coach Laing said, idly touching the whistle strung around her neck, "he's welcome to come. But from now on, he'll have to play by this coach's rules."

"You won't have to worry about that anymore." Tabby's tone grew serious. "Because Dad won't be showing up here. In fact, he doesn't want me to come either. He thinks I'm going to join the Castle Hill Cheerleaders."

Gasps and shocked exclamations echoed in the room.

"But Dad is wrong," Tabby said quickly. "I love being on the Cheer Squad. You guys are more than my friends—you're my family." Then she told about her bizarre encounter with Darlene and LaShaun.

"Those cheerleaders were spying on us?" Coach Laing asked in dismay when Tabby had finished. "That's terrible sportsmanship!"

"That's the way Darlene operates," Krystal said with a scowl. She lifted her poms and chanted, "Gimme a C-H-E-A-T—what does that spell? Darlene Dittman!"

Anna frowned. "She's gone too far."

"That's darned right," Krystal agreed with a vengeful gleam in her blue eyes. "We should get even by playing some nasty pranks on *her* squad."

"Any more talk like that and I'll fine you twenty jumping jacks!" Coach Laing gave Krystal a warning look. "There have been enough pranks."

"That's for sure." Tabby glanced down at her white sneakers. "Besides, Darlene may be dishonest, but she's not the saboteur."

"Are you sure?" Celine asked in an anxious voice.

"Absolutely."

"So who is the prankster?" Rachel asked with a puzzled lift of her dark brows.

"I don't know." Tabby sighed. "Darlene had the nerve to tease that it's an inside job."

"You mean one of us?" Anna asked in disbelief.

"That's what Darlene suggested," Tabby replied quietly.

Everyone was quiet for a moment, exchanging uneasy glances with each other.

Tabby rubbed her chin and looked around the room at her friends: Dedicated Wendi, dramatic Krystal, optimistic Anna, good-hearted Rachel, and sensitive Celine. A Cheer Squad member could find out Tabby's locker combination, have access to Wendi's E-mail, and borrow Coach Laing's office key. It almost made sense . . . almost.

One of us, Tabby thought with a shiver, *but which one?*

●●●●●●●●●●●

Eighteen

"I know who did it," Wendi told Tabby on the drive home. Wendi's mother had offered to drop Tabby off, and Tabby had readily agreed. It was more pleasant than dealing with her own mother, who continued to speak to her in an icily polite tone.

"You know who the saboteur is?" Tabby asked doubtfully. "Okay, so tell me."

"I'm surprised you haven't figured it out for yourself, Sherlock," Wendi said with a grin. "You're the one who said it might be someone on our squad."

"Technically I was just repeating what Darlene said—and we know how trustworthy she is." Tabby pointed out.

"But maybe she's right." Wendi leaned toward Tabby on the car seat. "The saboteur *has* to be someone close to us."

Tabby nodded, but her heart felt heavy. She hated to distrust her own friends.

"And there's only one Cheer Squad member who wants us out of the regionals," Wendi stated.

Tabby's mind flashed over the four names. Anna only saw the good side of people and was very enthusiastic about cheerleading. Krystal wanted to be an MTV star someday and loved to perform in public. Rachel was easygoing and seemed to have fun no matter what she was doing—which just left one person.

"Celine *is* hard to understand," Tabby admitted. "But I really enjoyed being with her at our sleepover."

"I did, too. Still, she's unpredictable and very moody. And she's not looking forward to the regionals."

"She's just nervous about competing against her former cheerleading friends." Tabby hesitated, testing the idea in her mind. She felt guilty for suspecting Celine, and yet the more she thought about it, the more it made sense. Celine *had* acted frightened of the pranks. She had even suggested they drop out of the regionals.

"Celine could be the saboteur," Tabby said slowly. "None of the pranks were dangerous—just annoying enough to scare us."

"I *was* a bit scared. It's spooky knowing someone is out to get you, but not knowing who, how, or when."

"Still, I can't believe Celine would break into Coach Laing's office and ruin our tape." Tabby turned her head, staring out her window at passing scenery: murky trees, dark buildings, rows of streetlights, and twinkling lights from cozy houses. Castle Hill looked like such a peaceful, friendly town—the sort of community where neighbors helped each other out and you could trust your friends.

But now I don't trust Celine, Tabby thought unhappily. *And suspicion feels like poison. . . .*

The car slowed down, turning onto Tabby's street. As it parked in front of a large apartment complex, Tabby grabbed her bag. "Thanks for the ride, Mrs. Holcroft," she said, opening her door.

"Any time, Tabby." Wendi's mother waved from the front seat.

"We'll confront you-know-who tomorrow at school," Wendi called out. "Everything will be fine. Then regional competition, here we come!"

"Yeah. I guess so." Tabby sighed, then turned and hurried up the apartment steps.

Opportunity plus motive equals Celine, Tabby told herself. *Case solved. And yet I'm bummed. I'm more worried about Celine's feelings than solving the mystery. Detectives have to uncover ugly truths that they would be happier never knowing. Playing detective was supposed to be fun, but it's not.*

When Tabby walked in her apartment, she saw Adam sitting at the kitchen table doing his homework and her mother spraying furniture polish on the coffee table.

"At last you're home," Mrs. Greene said, putting away her polish and rag. "We have to talk."

"Not another lecture," Tabby begged wearily. "I know I was inconsiderate to stay out late with Dad. I won't do it ever again. All right?"

"Not exactly." Her mother reached out and hugged Tabby. "Honey, I'm so sorry."

"You are?" Tabby's eyes widened with astonishment. This seemed to be an evening full of apologies. But she couldn't figure this one out. "Why? You didn't do anything wrong."

"That's where you're *wrong*." Mrs. Greene glanced at Adam, then added in a low voice, "Let's go into my bedroom where we can talk in private."

Tabby gave her mother a puzzled look as she followed her down the hallway. Her mother was using the same tone she had used three years ago when she broke the news about the divorce. Tabby's heart quickened and she fought the urge to cover her ears with her hands. She couldn't take any more bad news tonight.

Sitting on a cushioned cedar chest, Tabby looked up expectantly at her mother. "So, what's going on?"

Instead of answering, Mrs. Greene took a wrinkled piece of paper off her dresser top and handed it to Tabby. "Recognize this?"

Tabby stared at the familiar handwriting in shock. It was *her* handwriting—the letter she'd written to Wendi and decided not to send. "But I threw this away! How did you get it?"

"Whenever I'm upset, I clean. And the trouble with you and your dad put me in a major cleaning mood. So after I dropped you off at Castle Mansion, I scrubbed, vacuumed, and organized every corner of our apartment." She paused and flushed guiltily. "Including your room. I found the paper in your garbage."

"You read my private words?" Tabby cried in dismay.

"I did." Mrs. Greene nodded. "I wanted to make sure you hadn't accidentally thrown away a school lesson. But I was the one who got a lesson—about how my daughter feels. I had no idea you hoped your father and I would get back together."

"It was dumb. Kid stuff." Tabby looked away and shrugged. "Intellectually, I know you and Dad aren't compatible."

"We are very definitely not compatible," her mother said with a fond smile. "But that's our problem, not yours. I'm sorry that I made you feel like you had to choose between us. It's okay to love us both."

"I do." Tabby squeezed her mother's hand.

"Forgive me for snooping in your garbage?"

Tabby thought about how she had followed Darlene, read Mark's note, and spied on Darlene and LaShaun. "That's okay, Mom." Tabby grinned mischievously. "You couldn't help yourself. Snooping runs in our family."

Nineteen

Tabby tossed and turned in bed, trying to shut out the pitiful expression on Celine's face. "I didn't do it! I didn't do it!" Celine cried over and over.

Wendi floated into the picture and pointed a finger at Celine. "You are the saboteur. Confess and we'll forgive you."

Celine's black eyes were wild and she grabbed Tabby's hands and pleaded, "You believe me, don't you? Don't you?"

Tabby looked from Wendi to Celine, torn by doubt and confusion. "I want to believe you, Celine," Tabby said, half sobbing. "But all the evidence is against you and evidence doesn't lie—only people do."

Evidence doesn't lie. The words echoed ominously in Tabby's mind. *But what evidence?*

Tabby's eyes jerked open and she was surprised to find that it was morning. Her head ached and she felt a nagging sense of urgency—like there was something she should be doing.

"Evidence," she muttered, groggily getting out of bed and reaching for her clothes. "Is that the message of my dream?"

She shook her head and tried to clear her thoughts as she slipped into her stonewashed jeans. There was actually no evidence that proved Celine guilty—only a strong motive and plenty of opportunity.

"Maybe Wendi and I were jumping to conclusions about Celine," Tabby told herself. "I have no proof that she broke into my locker, left the E-mail, or ruined the tape."

Tabby walked over to her dresser and opened a bottom drawer. Carefully, she pulled out her only piece of real evidence—the Plum Berry Punch carton.

She took it to her desk and placed it under a bright lamp. It looked ordinary enough—a bit squished and sticky, but nothing weird.

"Wait a minute," she murmured. "This carton hasn't been opened. And yet it leaked all over my shoe. There must be a hole somewhere . . ."

Tabby dug into a desk drawer until she found a magnifying glass. Then she studied every inch of the carton. She couldn't detect fingerprints and the only marking was a store code and date on the carton bottom. But there had to be a hole somewhere!

Finally, Tabby found the hole—if she could call the tiny pinprick in the side of the carton a hole. The saboteur had simply punctured the carton and let gravity do the dirty deed. But the puncture mark was so small! How had enough juice to cover the bottom of a shoe dribbled out of such a micro-sized hole in only a few hours?

Tabby thought back to that day. She had assumed Darlene or LaShaun had placed the carton in her locker after lunch. That meant the juice would have had only about two hours to seep into the shoe. Was that long enough? Or had the carton been in her shoe much longer?

"I'll try an experiment," Tabby decided.

She remembered seeing some Plum Berry cartons in the kitchen cabinet. After the prank, she had avoided taking any to school. So unless Adam had drunk them, they were still there.

Feeling a renewed zest for detective work, Tabby hurried into the kitchen. Her mother and Adam were still asleep, so she tried not to slam the cupboards or make any other noise.

"Here they are!" she whispered, finding a package that had originally held six Plum Berry Punch cartons. Only two cartons remained—and Tabby grabbed them. Then she quickly left the kitchen and returned to her bedroom.

"Now for my supersleuth experiment," Tabby declared.

She dug into her closet for an old pair of sneakers, then placed one carton inside a ragged shoe. "I'll make the exact same pinprick hole in this carton and see how quickly it leaks," she decided with mounting excitement. Now *this* was investigating!

Lucky for me Mom buys the exact same drink that the saboteur used. Tabby thought as she looked around her room in search of some kind of pin. She found a safety pin and carefully punctured the side of the juice carton. Then she glanced at her bedside cat-shaped clock, glad that she didn't have to leave for school for an hour, and waited.

Five minutes passed and not one drop of juice leaked from the carton.

"And my hole is even bigger than the one the saboteur made," Tabby concluded with surprise.

Another five minutes passed ... ten ... fifteen ... seventeen ... and no telltale juicy drips.

"Maybe I need to shake the carton," Tabby muttered.

She reached for the carton and gave it a hard shake. One dark red drop of juice oozed out of the hole. "That's all? But that doesn't even cover a shoelace, much less the bottom of a shoe! That means the carton must have been in my sneaker for a long time ... more than two hours ... maybe the entire day!"

Tabby stared at both cartons. One was full of juice and the other was empty, and yet they looked nearly identical.

Suddenly Tabby noticed something about them that she hadn't noticed before—and instantly everything made sense.

Her mind raced, piecing together the fragments of the puzzle, each fact adding up to spell out one name.

There was no longer any doubt.

Tabby knew the exact identity of the saboteur.

●●●●●●●●●●●

Twenty

Tabby's mind was still spinning as she left her bedroom. Knowing who was guilty was one thing, but confronting that person was something else. She hoped she could handle it.

When she entered the kitchen, she saw that her brother had finally gotten up. Adam stood by the counter, spreading mayonnaise on four slices of white bread. He glanced at her with an impatient expression. "Hey, you seen the juice cartons?" he asked. "I'm making my lunch and I can't find them."

"At least we have plenty of bananas," Tabby teased, pointing to a bunch on the tiled countertop.

"Save the jokes for someone who isn't running late," Adam said as he slapped bologna on bread. "Just tell me where the drinks are."

"Only if you tell me something first." Swiftly, Tabby reached into a bag and withdrew the sticky sabotage carton. "Why did you do it?"

Adam jumped back a step and his jaw dropped.

"You can't prove anything. I don't know what you're talking about."

"Oh, yes, you do!" Tabby accused, turning the carton upside down and showing the coded print at the bottom. "Check out the store code and date."

"You're wasting my time."

"Somebody left this cartoon in my shoe. The stamped code is CA13 and the date is 2–97." Tabby whirled around and withdrew another Plum Juice carton from the bag. "And this drink also is coded CA13 and 2–97—the exact same."

"So?" Adam shrugged, but his cheeks deepened to a guilty shade of crimson.

"It came from *our* kitchen."

"Doesn't mean anything."

"Yes, it does." Tabby fixed Adam with a knowing stare. "It means that the saboteur is someone from my own family. And since I certainly didn't put a juice carton in my own shoe and I'm pretty sure Mom didn't leave it there either, that only leaves one person." Tabby shook her head sadly as she faced her brother. "Why did you do it, Adam?"

He shifted his feet and raked his fingers through his hair. "You can't prove ... oh, all right. Maybe I did pull a few pranks—but you deserved it."

"I did not!" Tabby's hand flew to her mouth.

"You stole Dad from me!" Adam said accusingly. "He missed a football practice and two wrestling meets. Do you know how it feels not to have any family supporting you?"

Tabby nodded, her anger fading to understanding.

"And then I find out Dad has been hanging out with you!" Adam continued. "And he didn't even stop by to talk to me. He'd rather be with you."

"So you played the pranks to get revenge?"

"Naw. You're way off base." He gave Tabby a dark look. "I left the juice carton and the E-mail message to scare you. I didn't want you to go to your competition."

"Why?" she asked softly.

"Because it's on the same Saturday as my benefit Winter Bowl football game. Dad helped organize this event and promised he'd go weeks ago. But he changed his mind when he heard about your dumb cheerleading contest. And I really want him to be there. Maybe it sounds dumb, but I count on Dad. I do better when I know he's out there cheering for me."

"So he's like a cheerleader for you," Tabby pointed out. "My sport isn't as dumb as you think. People feel better when someone's out there cheering for them."

"Guess you got me there." Adam flashed a reluctant grin. "It's hard not living with Dad anymore. But as long as we hung out together on weekends, it was okay—until he started hanging out with *you*."

"I know how you feel." Tabby gave Adam a sympathetic look. "Up until a week ago, Dad never paid *any* attention to me. I guess we just traded places."

"Well, it's not fair," Adam said roughly. "Maybe I was wrong to mess with your shoe and try to scare you with the E-mail, but I'd do it again if it would make Dad come to my football game."

Tabby couldn't help but smile. This was as

close to an apology as she'd get from Adam. Like their father, he hid any real feelings by acting macho.

"Okay, Adam. I forgive you," Tabby said, pointing her finger at his chest. "But we've got to deal with this. We have to let know Dad how we feel."

"I want him at my football game," Adam said firmly.

"And I want him at the regionals," Tabby replied. "He can't be in two places—two cities—at once, so he'll have to decide. I know! We'll take our demands to him in a contract."

"You got a weird way of thinking," Adam said with a chuckle. "Guess that's cause you're a brainiac. But a contract sounds cool."

"Good. We can work on it tonight."

"It's a deal. Now I gotta finish making my lunch. How about giving me one of our Plum Berry cartons."

Tabby hesitated, eyeing the carton with a safety-pin hole hidden in the side. But revenge wasn't her style, so she handed the only intact drink to Adam.

Then Tabby hurried to the phone to call Wendi and tell her that Celine was completely innocent.

●●●●●●●●●●●
*T*wenty-one

That afternoon at cheerleading practice, Tabby went to the front of the gym and asked everyone to gather around her. Then she explained the sabotage mystery to them.

Tabby enjoyed having solved the mystery. And she was really relieved that she and Wendi hadn't wrongly accused Celine. That was one part of the investigation that would remain a secret—forever.

"It was easy for your brother to leave the carton in your shoe and send the E-mail message, but I can't figure out how he ruined our tape," Wendi remarked as they did warm-up stretches. "He doesn't even go to our school."

"Now that you mention it, that is puzzling. I wish I'd asked Adam." Tabby paused in midstretch and considered this. Adam had his faults, but breaking and entering wasn't one of them. So how *had* he sabotaged Coach Laing's tape? Unable to come up with an answer, Tabby shrugged. "I guess I'll find out tonight—when Adam and I create a parenting contract."

"A *what?*" Wendi's auburn ponytail flopped over her shoulders as she turned to stare at her friend.

"It's my plan to help Dad be a better dad." Tabby chuckled, then explained while she stretched her arms from side to side.

Minutes later, Coach Laing blew her whistle and the Cheer Squad sprang into action. Wendi had come up with a creative twist on the musical opening. Instead of two three-girl line formations, they'd switch to three two-girl rows. Each girl would circle outward with her own best move: a grande jeté for Krystal, cartwheels for Anna, a toe-touch jump for Wendi, a round-off for Celine, sidesteps for Rachel, and an arabesque spin for Tabby.

"Really looking good!" Coach Laing beamed. "You girls work together well. I predict the regional competition audience will stand up and cheer for the Cheer Squad."

Tabby shared smiles with her teammates. *It's great to be here with my friends,* she thought. *Not even a first-place win could feel this good.*

Then everyone took their positions and practiced, practiced, practiced!

Tabby had to admit that without her father watching, the squad seemed to have more energy and enthusiasm. Still, Tabby missed her dad. And she found herself watching the door, half expecting it to burst open . . . but it never did.

Later at home, Tabby and Adam got together to write a parenting contract.

Tabby was pleasantly surprised how easy it was to work with Adam. They shared a lot of the same feelings and these feelings poured onto paper. Now all they had to do was present it to their father.

They got their chance the following evening.

Tabby had enjoyed another rousing Cheer Squad practice after school. It was Friday, which meant no homework, and she was looking forward to a soothing hot shower and several hours of relaxing reading. But her plans changed when she walked into her apartment and saw her father talking on the couch with Adam.

Adam looked relieved to see Tabby. But he greeted her with his usual gruff indifference. "It's about time."

Tabby dumped her backpack and duffle bag on a chair. "Hi, Adam." She hesitated and gulped uneasily. "Hi, Dad."

"I heard from Mr. Dittman that you refused to join his squad. Too bad." Mr. Greene shook his head regretfully. "Can't say I didn't try to help you."

"I would never say that. I appreciate all you've done. But I love the Cheer Squad." Tabby crossed her arms over her chest. "I belong there."

"The girls are okay. But I've never seen such a stubborn coach. She refused to listen to my ideas. She's too inexperienced and too darned young." He shrugged. "But it's not my concern anymore."

Tabby tensed. "What do you mean?"

"I won't sit by and watch you throw away your chance for success. If you won't accept my advice, I'm washing my hands of the booster club. And don't count on my being at your competition, either. I already told Adam I'd watch his football game."

Tabby frowned, fighting for control. She had

expected this, but that didn't stop it from hurting.

Adam gave his father a scathing look. "Dad, your attitude stinks!"

Tabby touched her ears, wondering if she needed her hearing checked. Adam was actually sticking up for her?

"Tabby's got a right to make her own decisions," Adam insisted. "Me, too."

Tabby flashed her brother a grateful look. His support gave her the courage to go to her backpack and withdraw a formal-looking document. "Dad, this is for you."

Mr. Greene pushed up his glasses on his nose as he took the typed paper. "Parenting contract? Who wrote this nonsense?"

"We both did," Adam answered. "Check out Item Number One."

Mr. Greene read out loud, "We the undersigned demand equal time and equal affection . . . Is this a joke?"

Sister and brother both shook their heads.

"Keep reading," Tabby said calmly.

"I have to call before I come over." Mr. Greene furrowed his brow. "You want twenty-four-hour notice if I have to cancel. You don't want me to make insulting comments about your mother. And you don't want me to criticize your coach. But I *never* criticize anyone!"

Tabby opened her mouth to differ, but Adam spoke first, "Yes, you do, Dad. The guys on my team even asked me to tell you to lay off Coach Conner. I just never had the nerve tell you before now."

Mr. Greene's shoulders sagged and he shook his head in disbelief. "This is crazy!"

"The way *you've* been playing games with *us* is crazy," Tabby replied.

"And unfair," Adam added. "All games need rules. You and Mom decided about the divorce, but we've been the ones getting penalized. So we're calling foul."

Mr. Greene looked at his kids, grimaced, then returned to the contract. He was quiet for a moment, as if realizing Tabby and Adam were serious. Finally, he lifted his head. "I gotta admit, you kids have some valid points. But I can't make any promises. A guy can't change overnight."

"We don't expect you to change, Dad." Tabby clasped his hand warmly. "We just want you to relax a bit and treat us fairly—love us the way we are."

"But I do!" he insisted, wrapping an arm around each one of them. "Okay, kids. You made your point. I only have one question."

Tabby wrung her hands on her lap. Was this the part where her father crumpled up the paper and stormed out the door? "What question?"

"Yeah, what?" Adam echoed uneasily.

Mr. Greene flashed a rueful smile. "Where do I sign?"

●●●●●●●●●●

Twenty-two

The next week passed quickly.

The Cheer Squad practiced every day, except for Wednesday, when they cheered at a basketball game. Tabby and her squad mates yelled, clapped, kicked, and waved poms in support of their Knights. And this time when Esteban dribbled the ball in the last quarter, his hoop shot resulted in a win.

Afterward, when Tabby went out for victory pizza, she sat beside her dad. Tabby was surprised how seriously her father was taking the parenting contract. And at home Adam was nicer, too. He insisted he hadn't destroyed the music tape, and Tabby believed him. But, if he hadn't done it, who had?

But there was no time to puzzle over this small mystery, because Saturday was C-Day—Competition Day!

"Do you have everything?" Mrs. Greene asked for the third or thirtieth time Saturday morning. Since Adam and Mr. Greene were going to the football game, Mrs. Greene offered to drive Tabby, Celine, and Celine's grandmother to the regionals. Tabby was thrilled her mother had been able to get the day off. And even better, in a few weeks Mrs. Greene would be starting a new, less demanding job.

Tabby grabbed her duffle bag. "I'm ready, Mom."

"Did you check to make sure you have everything?"

"Five times," Tabby said with a laugh. "Celine and Mrs. Jefferson are waiting to be picked up. Let's go already!"

The parking lot of Miramar High School was jam-packed.

"I can't believe so many people are here!" Tabby exclaimed, staring out the car window. She and Celine sat in the backseat while her mother and Celine's grandmother sat up front.

"Cheer competitions are big business," Celine said with a knowing grin. "Wait till you get into the auditorium. It'll be like sardine city."

"Ooh! Look at those girls wearing all black," Tabby exclaimed with mounting excitement as her mother slowed the car into a space. "There must be twenty girls in that squad!"

"Most squads are huge. My old squad had fifteen . . . Oh! There's Sherry now!" Celine pointed toward a bunch of girls wearing white one-piece uniforms with ribbons of orange across the skirt and down the long sleeves. And their squad name WILD TIGERS blazed across their backs.

"Which girl?" Tabby asked, unfastening her seat belt.

"The tall one with the long black braid."

"Want to go talk to her?"

"No . . . Not yet." Celine tapped her fingers idly against the car window. "This feels so weird. I used to cheer with Sherry and now I'm competing *against* her."

"You'll have a blast," Tabby said.

"I don't think so. If we do better than them, I'll feel bad. But if we do worse, I'll be embarrassed." Celine gave a heavy sigh. "I lose either way."

"What a lame attitude. It doesn't matter who wins. Your friends—new and old—will still be your friends."

"I hope so," Celine said—but she didn't sound convinced.

A short time later, Tabby spotted Coach Laing, Wendi, and the other Cheer Squad girls by the sign-up table in the doorway of the auditorium.

When Wendi noticed Tabby, she made her way through the crowd and hurried over. "We're all signed up!" Wendi said with shining gray eyes. "There are six junior high squads competing in the performance cheer division. We go on fifth— after the Castle Hill Cheerleaders."

Tabby clutched her hands together. "*After* Darlene's group?"

Wendi nodded. "At least we're not last. That lucky spot goes to a group called the Wild Tigers."

"That's Celine's San Jose group." Tabby's gaze swept over to Celine, who stood in a corner practicing arm motions with Rachel.

"I'm so hyped about competing. Everything is incredible!" Wendi marveled. "I've never seen so many cheerleaders."

"Look at those high-school girls on the grass," Tabby said, pointing to an open quad area where nearly two dozen girls in yellow and white gathered. "They're working on a stunt. Wow! Did you see how high they tossed that flier?"

"Did I ever!" Wendi gave a low whistle. "I'm glad we're in the junior group and don't have to compete against *that* squad. I bet they've been cheerleading for years."

"And check out those girls." Tabby gestured toward three girls heading for the sign-in desk. "I love how their hair is pulled back in bouncy ringlets and silver-blue scrunchies."

"Cool!" Wendi cried enviously. "I wish we'd done that!"

Tabby grinned. "Maybe next time."

"If we score high enough, next time will be a major competition," Wendi declared. "The nationals!"

Tabby's head spun. Was Wendi just dreaming or would the Cheer Squad really compete at a national event someday? It was an awesome thought ... but very exciting.

Swarms of people filled the hallway and poured into the auditorium. Tabby's mother was already inside, sitting with the other Cheer Squad parents and friends in the crowded bleachers. Three walls were lined with bleachers: one for spectators and two for cheerleaders.

After changing into their green-and-gold uniforms, Tabby followed Wendi to the cheerleader bleachers, where they would wait with their squad until it was time to get ready to perform.

"There's Darlene Dittman," Wendi whispered,

pointing to the top row. "And check out her uniform!"

Tabby's gaze shot upward. Darlene's squad wore the school colors green and gold in a dazzling style: the front was a solid glittery gold and the back was a Day-Glo green.

"Mega-awesome uniforms," Tabby exclaimed.

"Like something you'd see on MTV. Don't stare at them too long or you might go blind," Wendi teased. Then she gave Tabby a look. "You could have joined the Castle Hill squad. Then you'd be wearing an expensive glow-in-the-dark uniform, too. Do you regret sticking with us?"

"No way!" Tabby struck a model-like pose. "I love my uniform—gold and green blended in a simple, classy style. It's perfect."

"Tabby! Wendi! Over here," Coach Laing called out. It was hard to hear over the multitude of voices, but Tabby made out the words, "Squad meeting."

Tabby and Wendi joined their squad mates in a huddle around their coach.

"Okay, girls," Rusty Laing began in a hyped tone. "Here are my three rules of competition: One, always smile. Two, do your best. And three, have fun."

"Gimme a F-U-N!" Krystal spelled out. "I'm already having tons of fun! I can't wait to get out there and cheer."

"Me, too," Wendi said with a huge grin.

"I'm so glad we're here," Anna added.

"This is a special day for all of us." Coach Laing grinned. "Any minute the competition will begin. But before I explain performance procedure, I

want to tell you something else ... something
you may have wondered about."

"What?" Tabby tilted her head curiously.

"It has to do with the ruined tape." Coach
Laing pushed back her auburn-streaked bangs.
"I found out who destroyed it."

●●●●●●●●●●●

Twenty-three

Tabby stared in astonishment at her coach. "WHO?"

Coach Laing pointed across the large bustling room to the other bleachers where family and friends sat. "Someone who's over there." The beads in her braids rustled as she gave a rueful shrug. "My six-year-old niece, Jancee."

"You're kidding!" Krystal exclaimed. "Why would a little kid play a prank on us?"

"It wasn't a prank," Coach Laing said quickly. Then she went on to explain how her niece, who had been celebrating her birthday, wanted to "pretend" cheerleader with her friends. So Jancee "borrowed" the tape from her aunt's purse, but ended up accidentally ruining it. And it had taken Jancee a week to work up the courage to confess and apologize to her aunt.

Tabby smiled over the story. At last, the final mystery was solved. *Now the only mystery left,* Tabby thought, *is how well our squad will do today.*

A hush settled over the audience when a balding man wearing an official-looking jacket leaned into a microphone and cleared his throat.

The regional competition was beginning!

There were nearly a dozen different divisions, split up between junior high, junior varsity, and varsity. First up was the show cheer division, starting with a varsity group called the Apaches. Applause rocked the bleachers, music echoed off the walls, and ten girls wearing red and white uniforms enthusiastically ran to the center floor.

The next hour was mind-boggling. So many rousing cheers, tumbling moves, impressive stunts, and dance steps. Fantastic!

And then it was time for the Cheer Squad to leave the bleachers. As they filed to the warm-up area, Tabby watched the first group in her division, the Mustangs, strut onto the floor dressed in a western theme; denim skirts, suede vests, and checkered scarfs around their necks. But when one girl snagged a scarf during a lift, she fell down and the audience gasped. Fortunately, she was caught by a quick-acting spotter. Tabby felt sorry for the Mustang cheerleader.

Two more squads performed in the junior performance cheer division. One was good, the other was less than good.

The fourth squad announced was the Castle Hill cheerleaders. Tabby watched them run onto the floor, then break into a funky jazz sequence. The Castle Hill squad *had* improved. Darlene's hand motions were smoother and LaShaun was only slightly out of sync. And when they turned around, the dramatic two-colored uniforms were striking.

"They're looking good," Wendi whispered to Tabby. "Although Darlene is still acting like a prima donna—like her moves are the only ones that matter."

Tabby nodded, noticing how Darlene swept her arms out after a spin, nearly slapping LaShaun, who lagged a half beat behind.

"They're getting into position for a double basket toss," Wendi commented, standing on her toes for a better view. "Kayla and LaShaun are bases. Good transition moves. And now Darlene is climbing to Kayla's and LaShaun's shoulders. . . ." Wendi paused. "Am I seeing things, or did Darlene kick LaShaun in the head?"

Tabby frowned. She had noticed the same thing, but couldn't believe Darlene would be so inconsiderate. It was a relief when the Castle Hill squad finished.

"Next up," the announcer boomed, "the Cheer Squad!"

"This is it! Listen to the crowd cheer . . . for us!" Wendi exclaimed, jumping up and swishing her poms.

"This is so exciting!" Tabby cried, glad that her mother was part of the applause—two hands clapping just for her.

And then the Cheer Squad was on.

Familiar music rocked the auditorium as Tabby lined up behind Wendi. With golden poms in the air, Tabby gracefully ran into the center floor with her squad mates, getting into their opening formation. In two-girl rows, the girls moved forward, then split off into dynamic tumbling and dance steps, until all six girls blended back together in one long kick line. The line swiveled, bending and breaking off into new, dramatic steps.

Thunderous applause became part of Tabby's soul, and she smiled proudly. She was not just one person. She was part of a squad—one-sixth of a special group.

The music portion of the routine ended and the Cheer Squad held out their poms and shivered them so they shimmered like a mass of golden leaves on a breezy autumn day.

Then the chants began:

> *Move it, work it!*
> *Go, Knights! Go!*
> *Our team is the best!*
> *They can't be stopped!*
> *Move it, work it!*
> *The Knights can't be topped!*

On the word "topped," Tabby sprang up on the bases' shoulders into a lift.

> K-N-I-G-H-T-S
> *Knights!*
> *The team with energy to burn!*
> *They'll strive to win!*
> *With every turn!*

Tabby waved her poms high from her position at the top of the lift and slowly the bases turned, making a complete circle, which Tabby finished by springing forward and dismounting with a half twist.

The crowd cheered, stomped, and whistled, and

when the Cheer Squad finished, Tabby felt exhilarated.

After Tabby and her friends filed offstage, they hugged each other, squealed, and jumped excitedly. Coach Laing joined them and they all hugged, squealed, and jumped some more.

Finally, they settled down on the bleachers and watched the other squads perform.

"Those are my friends from San Jose!" Celine exclaimed, pointing to the Wild Tigers.

"They're doing great," Tabby said. "How about you?"

"I talked with Sherry before we went on. It was terrific to see her. And I realized it doesn't matter who does better." Celine's black eyes sparkled. "In fact, I hope her squad wins big." Then she giggled. "Of course, I hope we win big, too,"

"It would be nice," Tabby admitted with a grin. "We'll find out in a few hours. Now all we can do is wait and enjoy the rest of the show."

The coed division was the last to go on. Tabby admired how the boys on the squad could propel the fliers high in the air. Most of the guys just stood around for lifts and stunts, but a few were skilled gymnasts and dancers.

"Those guys are something else," Tabby murmured to Wendi.

"You said it," Wendi replied enthusiastically. "Boys on a squad really help a routine. I can see why Darlene tried to pay Mark and T.J. to join her squad. Only she asked the wrong guys."

Tabby nodded, then returned her gaze to the center floor.

Finally, all the squads had performed. It had

taken over four hours and Tabby's stomach was starting to grumble. She was eager to dive into the lunch that the parent booster club had prepared. But first—the competition results.

Dozens of cheerleaders gathered on the center floor with their squads. Tabby guessed that each squad with their bright uniforms must resemble a colorful quilt from the bleachers.

"They're announcing the results of *our* division!" Wendi cried anxiously, clutching Wendi's hand.

Tabby nodded, so excited she could barely breathe. She knew that all six squads in the junior performance cheer division would receive some kind of award: trophies for first, second, and third, and certificates for the rest. A certificate would be fine, but Tabby couldn't help but hope for a trophy.

"In the junior category," the balding, short announcer rang out, "certificates of achievement go out to the Grace Gophers, West Creek Cougars, and the Mustangs."

Applause erupted and a girl from each squad came up to accept a gold-inscribed certificate.

"Now for third place," the announcer resumed moments later. "The third-place winners are the Castle Hill Cheerleaders!"

Tabby clapped, genuinely happy her rival team had done well. But a glance at Darlene showed that the blond squad captain was far from happy. Her smile was stiff as she trudged up to accept her squad's award. She didn't even say thank you when a woman handed her a gold trophy.

"What a poor sport," Wendi whispered to

Tabby. "I guess Darlene isn't satisfied with anything but first place."

Tabby nodded, ashamed that someone from her own school let winning be the only goal. Didn't Darlene know how to have fun?

"Now for second place," the announcer boomed.

Tabby squeezed Wendi's hand.

"The second place winners are . . ." The announced paused. "THE CASTLE HILL CHEER SQUAD!"

"That's us!" Tabby exclaimed joyously. "Wow! We won!"

All around her, Tabby's squad mates jumped, squealed, and threw up their poms with excitement. Second place! What an honor! And watching Wendi proudly accept a trophy was thrilling.

Finally, first place went to the San Jose Wild Tigers. Tabby glanced over at Celine and saw the largest, happiest smile she had ever seen from her unpredictable friend.

"Want to hold our trophy?" Wendi asked, showing off the foot-long gleaming golden statue of a cheerleader. Engraved on the base were the words: SECOND PLACE WINNER, JUNIOR PERFORMANCE CHEER, REGIONAL COMPETITION.

"I'd love to hold it!" Tabby cried, carefully lifting the surprisingly heavy trophy. It felt cool, smooth, and wonderful. "So who's going to keep it?"

"Who else?" Wendi pushed back her auburn ponytail. "Coach Laing."

Tabby nodded. It was the perfect choice.

"Can I hold it?" Krystal begged.

"Me, too," Anna added.

"We want a turn!" Celine and Rachel said in unison.

"This little golden cheerleader is *very* popular," Tabby said with a chuckle.

"I've got an idea," Wendi said with a sudden gleam in her gray eyes. "Listen up, everyone."

Tabby gave her friend a curious glance. There was a strange excitement to Wendi's tone. Something big was up.

"After watching the competition today," Wendi stated, "I decided we were missing something from our squad."

"Missing what?" everyone asked.

"Not *what. Who.*" Wendi flashed a mischievous grin. "We need more cheerleaders. But not ordinary cheerleaders—tall, strong, hunky cheerleaders. I think we should invite *boys* to join our squad."

If you enjoyed Cheer Squad #3: Stand Up and Cheer!,
sample the following brief selection from

CHEER SQUAD #4:
BOYS ARE BAD NEWS

coming from Avon Camelot in January 1997.

"Gimme a B! Gimme an O! Gimme a Y!" Krystal Carvell chanted, jumping up and moving her arms from side-to-side. Grinning at her five Cheer Squad teammates, she yelled, "What's that spell?"

"BOY!" Wendi Holcroft's reply was the most enthusiastic as she looked up from the gym floor where she tied her sneaker laces. "And, oh, boy! Do we ever need one!"

"Not just one," practical Tabby Greene pointed out, zipping her duffle bag closed and smoothing away wrinkles from her green warm-up jacket. "We'll need at least two boys to balance out our routines."

"One, two, five, ten, a dozen! The more guys the better!" Krystal laughed and pushed her long blond ponytail over her shoulders. She was the most dramatic of the cheerleaders, and she was proud of it. Someday she planned to be a dazzling

MTV star—so funky and far-out that even Madonna would blush.

Anna Herrera, Krystal's best friend, gave Krystal a supportive look. "It'll be great to have boys for extensions, basket tosses, and pyramids. They can really shoot a flyer like me high in the air. I'm so glad Wendi decided to recruit boy cheerleaders."

"That's the plan anyway," squad captain Wendi said in a more serious tone. She pointed toward the front of the gym where the squad's young, energetic coach, Rusty Laing, sorted through some papers. "I've already run the idea by Coach Laing and she's all for it. Now we just have to find some athletic guys who want to join the Cheer Squad."

Join in the team spirit from the

#1: CRAZY FOR CARTWHEELS
78438-6/$3.99 US/$4.99 Can

Wendi! Tabby! Krystal! Anna! They're the best they can be at kicks and cartwheels, but they never had a chance when they tried out for the Castle Hill Cheerleaders. Only the coach's daughter and her obnoxious friends were picked.

#2: SPIRIT SONG
78439-4/$3.99 US/$4.99 Can

The new Cheer Squad has come a long way in just a short time. With Wendi as squad captain and Anna's aunt as their advisor, Cheer Squad has more than lived down the "loser" tag the Castle Hill Cheerleaders tried to pin on them.

#3: STAND UP AND CHEER!
78440-8/$3.99 US/$4.99 Can

With a great coach, new routines and plenty of enthusiasm, the Cheer Squad is sure they can win the state regionals. The trouble is, Tabby's football coach dad insists on helping the squad win, and his interference is causing trouble with the squad's coach and Tabby's teammates.

Coming Soon

#4: BOYS ARE BAD NEWS   78441-6/$3.99 US/$4.99 Can

1641